THE ALPHA'S SURRENDER

L.E. WILSON

EVERBLOOD
PUBLISHING

ALSO BY L.E. WILSON

Deathless Night Series (The Vampires)

A Vampire Bewitched

A Vampire's Vengeance

A Vampire Possessed

A Vampire Betrayed

A Vampire's Submission

A Vampire's Choice

The Kincaid Werewolves (The Werewolves)

Lone Wolf's Claim

A Wolf's Honor

The Alpha's Redemption

A Wolf's Promise

A Wolf's Treasure

The Alpha's Surrender

The Sergones Coven (Dragon Shifters & Vampires)

Fire of the Dreki

Blood of the Master

Mature & Desired (Angsty Seasoned Contemporary)

Be With Me

le@lewilsonauthor.com

ISBN:978-1-945499-29-6

Print Edition

Publication Date: June 23, 2020

Editor: Jinxie Gervasio @ jinxiesworld.com

CHAPTER 1

Cedric waited inside the cabin with Lucian and Keelin and wondered—again—how everyone had been aware of Lucian's secret hidey-hole except for him.

He was the alpha. There should be no secrets between him and the shifters he was responsible for. What if something had happened and he'd needed to find Lucian? Or the pup had gotten hurt while he was out here and the others were gone and Cedric didn't know where to find him?

How the fook was he supposed to protect his family if they hid things from him?

A low growl emanated in the center of his chest and he released the tension on a long exhale. Lucian had always been a crabbit beast, fighting Cedric's dominance over him every time he turned around. At least until the young one had mated Keelin. The lass was not only The Key and the most important element to keeping the soul suckers locked away in their own dimension, but she was also the one responsible for single-handedly taming the demons inside of Lucian.

And that made Cedric's job a hell of a lot easier.

A low growl rumbled through the silent room, one not of his making this time, and Cedric realized he was smiling gratefully at the lass who currently filled his thoughts.

She smiled in return before running a soothing hand over her irate mate's back, soothing his possessive grumblings.

The storm raging in Lucian's blue-gray eyes tempered down to a minor squall at her touch, and he grabbed her hand and kissed the back of her knuckles before shooting Cedric an apologetic glance for threatening him.

Cedric narrowed his eyes in warning, but to be honest, he didn't take offense. Much. Wolves were extremely territorial, especially over their mates. And Lucian, a wolf who ran a wee bit hotter than the others, took this to an extreme.

The door opened and a male nearly as tall as Cedric with long, wavy brown hair and a short beard ducked through the opening. His bright blue eyes quickly cased the place before he reached back and took the hand of a female to assist her inside. She stumbled over the doorstep, but he was ready, catching her easily and grinning when a heated blush rose up her neck to color her cheeks. Gently, he brushed her golden brown locks from her face and hugged her against his side as he pulled them out of the way so the others behind her could come in.

Marc entered in much the same way Brock had, his dark eyes landing on Cedric and waiting for his nod before he stepped fully inside. Turning, he gave a smile of encouragement to his Bronaugh as she followed him into the small cabin. The lass tucked a strand of wheat-blond hair behind her ear with her free hand. The other held tight to her mate's arm. Cedric was relieved to see her eyes flashed no colors, but were a warm brown, much like her mate's.

Marc closed the door behind them and they took a seat on the bed, the only piece of furniture in the place other than a small table and chairs in the kitchen area and a wood stove near the door.

The only ones missing were Duncan and Ryanne.

Although summer was fast approaching and the sun was rising through the trees, Cedric had closed the curtains over the single window when he, Lucian, and Keelin had gotten there, and with the door closed it took his eyes a partial second to adjust to the dim light. When they did, he walked to the entry of the kitchen, then turned to face the somber group.

"Thank ye all for meeting me here. I did no' want tae take a chance o' the prince overhearing any o' this."

There were a few curious looks, but no one raised any questions. Cedric looked at each of the lasses in turn. They were all Fae: one sweet and pure, one besieged by the sinister magic of the *an olc*, and one a little of both. He allowed his gaze to wander back to Bronaugh. "Can I trust all o' ye?" Although the question was meant for all of them, he directed it toward her in particular. He held nothing against her for her heritage, but there was something happening with the lass, and his gut told him it wasn't only the natural progression of her dark nature she was battling.

"You can trust me," she told him. "I'm not thrilled with what has happened with my people. But I am loyal to Marc above all else. I would never do anything that would put him in harm's way."

Something about her words struck Cedric as a wee bit... off, but for now, he only needed her reassurance she would not go off the deep end anytime soon. He gave her a nod and turned to the others. Heather was the only one who was of the *na maithe* tribe. And although she was raised on the other side of the world with humans, as a "daughter" of the Faerie prince, she was the next biggest risk. "What aboot ye, Heather? Tell me now if ye feel any sort o' protective feelings for yer prince. None o' us will blame ye for them, but I dinna want ye here if ye do, for yer own protection."

Brock frowned and searched his mate's expression as though the idea had never occurred to him.

But she only gave Cedric a quick shake of her head. "He's only my prince as far as he needs to be to keep me off of his radar. After the little game he played with our lives—solely for his own amusement no matter what he may say—I believe he's more crazy than anything. I am one hundred percent behind you. It's time he was removed from the position of protector of our people. A position he never should have had to begin with."

Cedric didn't miss the meaningful glance she sent to the other females. "The biggest thing I've learned since meeting all of you is that we are all Fae. It doesn't matter what tribe or where or how we were raised. Soul suckers aside, there's no reason for any animosity between us, and I think it's Prince Nada who's been feeding that opinion for a long time." She looked at the others again. "Am I wrong?"

"No," Keelin told her. "I don't think you are." She smiled at Heather, then at Bronaugh, before turning her attention back to Cedric. "What do you need to tell us? I can guarantee you it won't leave this room."

Satisfied with their answers, he apologized to their males. "I'm sorry I had tae go there, and did no' warn ye ahead o' time, but I needed tae be sure yer lasses spoke the truth."

"It's all right," Marc said. "What's going on? Why did ye need tae bring us way out here?"

Cedric linked his hands behind his back and grinned. "I have a bit o' good news for ye. And again, allow me tae apologize for no' being honest with ye until now. But I heard from Duncan. He is alive and well, and so is Ryanne."

That last was nearly drowned out by the whoops and hollers and howls of the pack. Marc stood from the bed, pulling Bronaugh with him, and swung her around as he hugged her close. Brock bent forward with his hands on his knees as Heather pounded him on the back with enthusiasm. When he straightened, they both grinned at each other until their faces looked about to crack.

His heart full at their reactions, Cedric turned to Lucian and Keelin. The lass had a knowing smile on her face, and he knew she was not surprised at all. For he'd recently found out Ryanne and Keelin had long been friends, and this is why Ryanne had been sneaking around in the woods behind her house when Duncan first saw her.

However, as far as Prince Nada was concerned, no one knew of Duncan and Ryanne's whereabouts or even if they still lived. Upon Cedric's orders, every wolf for miles around had been brought in to help find them. Search parties had been patrolling for weeks, combing every inch of the mountains within a hundred mile radius. It was a waste of resources, but necessary if they wanted to convince the Fae prince that he and his pack were oblivious to his secrets.

And to keep up with the charade, all contact between Duncan and the pack had been cut off so there wasn't any chance of their communication being intercepted.

"When did ye hear from him?" Lucian asked.

"Aboot a week ago." Turning to Lucian, he didn't expect the amount of enthusiasm the others were showing. Lucian and Duncan had always been at odds, with the older wolf being the bane of Lucian's existence, having a habit of teasing the younger wolf until he was right ready to rip him limb from limb.

Of course, it was for Lucian's own good. It had taught him to control his beast enough that it was relatively safe to have him around.

So, it was a shock to the alpha to find tears in the lad's stormy gray eyes. "Tis okay, Lucian. Truly. Duncan is alive and well and safe. As is Ryanne."

Lucian crossed his muscular arms over his wide chest. "Why are ye only telling us this now? It's been months, Cedric. Months that ye let us go on fearin' the worst."

"Lucian…" Keelin rubbed his back again. And aye, Cedric could see the muscles shifting beneath the thin cotton of his T-shirt from where he stood.

"Do NO' try tae stand up for him, Keelin," Lucian growled at her.

Cedric held up his hand, stopping whatever she'd been about to say. "Dinna say it, Keelin. Lucian is right. I should no' have lied tae him. Should no' have lied tae all of ye," he said to the group at large. "But I did no' have a choice."

"Ye had a choice," Lucian gritted out.

"No' if I did no' want the Faerie prince pullin' the truth out o' yer heads like he did tae Duncan. Aye." He nodded at the shocked expressions surrounding him. "That's what he did. Pulled Ryanne's existence right from his head without a word spoken between them. I saw it with me own eyes."

The lasses exchanged a few looks between them, but Cedric noticed they didn't share in the surprise of their mates.

"Why didn't you tell us he could do that?" Brock asked Heather.

She shrugged. "I'd heard rumors, but I wasn't positive they were true. You know how things get built up."

"It's no' the lass's fault," Cedric told them. "How are they tae ken what the daft prince is going tae do?"

"So, where is Duncan? And Ryanne?" Marc asked.

Cedric weighed the pros and cons of telling them. When he and Brock had first brought them home, the two of them had stayed right here in this very cabin until Cedric could set up a new place away from the pack where they'd be safe, unbeknownst to the rest of the pack for their own safety. When he had a place, he'd spirited them away in the dead of the night. It was not the pack's way to keep secrets from each other, but it was the only way he knew to keep them all out of the prince's hands.

Prince Nada didn't know Cedric and Brock had saved Ryanne. And he also wasn't aware that Ryanne had then gone back to the caves and saved Duncan. As far as Cedric could tell from the conversations they'd had, the prince thought his daughter was dead and Duncan had either joined her or was in no state of mind to free himself from the land of his nightmares.

The Faerie prince was a wily one, and Cedric would not take any chances with Duncan's life. Or Ryanne's. He didn't want to give the prince any reason to suspect they weren't telling him the truth when the pack said they didn't know where they were. He didn't want him pulling anything else from anyone's head. He needed the pack and the surrounding wolves to believe Duncan and his Fae lass were gone, and to react accordingly, both physically and emotionally.

As he'd predicted, the prince had come around often at first, playing his games, asking a lot of questions about Duncan's whereabouts, and if any of them had seen Ryanne or Thomas's wolves, who'd also gone missing.

Once or twice, the prince had focused a little too hard on Cedric's responses, and he'd felt his royal pain in the arse probing around in his head like a worm. However, Cedric wasn't the alpha for no reason, and he'd been prepared. The prince could poke around in there all he wanted, he would find nothing but the latest binge-worthy series on Netflix or an honest concern for his missing wolf and his mate, because even though he'd arranged their disappearance, even he didn't know where they were or what was happening with them.

He and the others did their part, unknowingly as it was, and exuded genuine fear and grief. And after a few weeks, the prince's visits tapered off. He was no longer interested in what the rest of the pack was doing, and didn't waste his time questioning Cedric on whether or not any progress had been made in their search.

However, Cedric was no fool. He was quite sure the prince still watched the wolf's activities. And to that effect, he kept up the daily and nightly patrols and check-ins. And that seemed to keep him satisfied.

But, aye. After waiting one more week to be certain, it was time to fill in the others. "Duncan and Ryanne are in a safe house, borrowed from one o' the other packs. They're laying low for now."

"What pack?" Brock asked.

"Oregon," Cedric told them. "I can no' tell ye any more than that. Because tae be honest, I dinna even ken exactly where they are. Only Mack, the alpha in those parts, can tell ye that. And he's been sworn tae secrecy." He looked at each face in turn. "'Twas the only way tae keep him safe, ye ken that?"

"Aye," Marc answered. "I do. And so does everyone else, even if they will no' admit tae it." Looking straight at Lucian, he lifted both eyebrows.

"I ken," Lucian growled. "Even if I do no' agree."

His temper rose, white-hot and unexpected, and Cedric whirled on him. "What else would ye have had me do," he bit out. "'Twas the only way I could think o' tae keep the prince from sniffing around here."

"Maybe no' lying tae us would have been a good start," Lucian growled.

"Let it go, Lucian. This isn't getting us anywhere," Bronaugh said.

Lucian's upper lip lifted off as he flashed his canines at her. He took a step toward her, but Keelin pulled him back.

With a roll of her eyes, Bronaugh looked at Cedric. "So, what do we do from here?"

Linking his hands behind his back, Cedric paced back and forth across the floor, rolling his shoulders and stretching his neck as he got his temper under control. He was letting Lucian get to him when he needed to keep a cool head. "The prince came tae me with an idea before all o' this happened, and the more I think on it, the more I'm starting tae agree with him." He stopped pacing and faced the others. "We need tae keep Duana under control, especially with what we all ken now aboot her and the prince."

"What idea is that?" Brock asked. Though his words were calm, Cedric didn't miss the way he tightened his grip on

Heather. And he didn't blame the lad. Anything to do with the Faerie prince made him nervous.

Cedric took a deep breath. "He wants me tae mate Duana."

"Are ye mad, Cedric?"

"Ye can no'!"

"Are you crazy?"

Bronaugh's eyes flashed with bright pinks and greens and yellows.

"Haud yer wheesht!" Cedric cut them off. "Just calm the fook down. I'm no' going tae do it for real. I'm only going tae tell the prince I am." He waited until he had everyone's attention again. "I've given it lots o' thought. Tis the only way tae find out what she's up tae. Because we all know it canna be anything good." He held up a finger for each point. "One. We need tae find out why she was snooping around Keelin's house. Two..."

"That's easy," Lucian said. "We ken now she's the prince's daughter. But, unlike Ryanne, she's as daft as he is. And now that we ken what his true plan is—tae release the Dark Fae and kill off the rest o' us—it's easy tae see. She wanted tae get rid of Keelin so she couldn't tighten the lock on the portal, because it's the same thing she's been blatherin' on aboot."

Keelin, who had been quiet up till now, stepped forward. "I don't think that's it. Or, at least, not all of it. And I don't like this idea Cedric. You need to stay away from her. Duana is more dangerous than you know."

"Och, no." He smiled to soften his abrupt dismissal of her concern. "I appreciate the concern, lass. But it's the only way tae get tae her." His chest swelled when he thought about the intriguing musk that hovered around the princess whenever she was around him. "She's sweet on me, and I'm no' saying that tae be boastful. I can tell by the colors in her eyes whenever she's near me." He would've mentioned the scent that came from the lass also, but didn't want to discuss such sensitive matters in front of the females.

"Are ye sure it's no' because she's angry?" Marc raised one eyebrow. "Because I get that a lot." He grinned as Bronaugh shoved him.

Cedric had to admit he had a point. "Aye, sometimes she is," he conceded. "But no' all the time. The other times, ye see, I ken it's because she's attracted tae me." He tapped the side of his nose discretely.

The wolves nodded in understanding.

"Do you really think you have a chance to get close to her without her getting suspicious?" Bronaugh asked.

"I think I do," he said in all seriousness, as visions of Duana's soft curves bared to his hungry gaze swam through his head. "Aye, I think I do."

CHAPTER 2

In downtown Seattle, not far from SeaTac airport, Cedric walked up to the door of the prince's house and raised his fist to knock. He pulled his hand back before his knuckles could touch the wood.

Voices came from within, raised in anger. No, it was only one voice in particular he recognized, and the anguish ringing within it caused his heart to pound and his wolf to surge beneath his skin.

"You're crazy. Do you know that?" Duana yelled. "How can you ask that of me?"

Someone—the daft prince, he would assume—mumbled something Cedric couldn't quite catch due to the ridiculously loud exhaust of a passing truck. He leaned in as it passed, hoping the person would say more, and this time he recognized the silvery tones. It was the Faerie prince she was yelling at, for sure.

He waited another minute to see if he could catch anything

else, but when nothing more was said he knocked firmly, three times.

The door swung open wide, and Prince Nada stood just on the other side. Cedric hadn't even heard footsteps approach, and the tiny hairs on the back of his neck stood straight up at his sudden appearance.

Dressed in his typical ensemble all the way down to his silver-tipped boots, his black suit was wrinkle-free as though he never sat down, his long silver hair was immaculately combed, and his silver-tipped cane was in his free hand.

Apparently dressing down was not something he did at home.

"You're right on time!" the prince exclaimed with a grin on his face so wide you would think they were long lost friends and hadn't just seen each other a few weeks before.

"I dinna ken ye were expecting me," Cedric answered. He even managed to hide the sarcasm from his tone. Sort of.

"Oh, but I knew you were coming. I felt it in my bones. Come in! Come in!" Stepping out of the way, Prince Nada swung out the arm holding the cane, nearly knocking a vase off its table in his exuberance to welcome his guest.

Cautiously, Cedric stepped over the threshold, ducking his head so as not to hit the top of the doorframe. Inside, he felt the need to do the same, the small rooms and seven foot ceilings closing in on him.

The prince's house looked the same as it had the last time he was there. Sparsely furnished with little furniture, other than a couple of chairs in the main living room, it was dark and gloomy even as the sun was going down, for there were few windows, the panes covered in cheap blinds and thick curtains.

Apparently, all of the glamour was saved for the back bedroom that housed his and Duana's thrones.

Over the prince's shoulder, Cedric saw one small improvement. He'd finally gotten a small, white kitchen table and chairs. Whereas before there had only been barstools along the counter.

But the appearance of the table barely broke through his consciousness, for Duana stood in the doorway to the kitchen.

At the sight of her, his heart, which had only just calmed its rapid pounding, skipped a few beats before picking up its pace. Unlike the prince, she was dressed more comfortably in tight, black knit pants and a short-sleeve, mossy-green pullover shirt. Fluffy slippers were on her feet, and her long dark hair was piled on top of her head, showing off her elegant neck.

She had stilled when she'd seen him standing there, just inside the front door. "What are you doing here?" she asked.

The prince waved one hand in her direction, as though to shoo her away. "He's not here to see you," he said.

At her father's immediate dismissal, colors flashed in her eyes as they landed on the prince.

"Och, but I am," Cedric said. "I'm here tae see if Duana would like tae go tae dinner with me."

The complete and utter silence following his statement was the loudest thing he'd ever heard, and Cedric shifted his weight uncomfortably.

When he'd come up with the idea back at his apartment, after thinking of and discarding a hundred other scenarios, it had seemed like a grand idea at the time. Why not just ask her out as a way to announce his intentions? Not make a big deal about it. Prince Nada, himself, wanted him to do it.

And perhaps Cedric was not as opposed to the idea as he let on.

He was about to rescind his invitation, thinking maybe the prince had changed his mind, when the crazy loon smiled. "Of course, she would!" he told Cedric.

"No, I wouldn't," the princess contradicted.

Stepping around the prince and focusing his attention on her, Cedric asked, "But why no'? Aren't ye hungry?"

"I already ate," she stated.

"No, she didn't," the prince said. "She was just telling me a couple of minutes ago how starving she was."

"See?" Cedric gave her what he hoped was a convincing smile. "Ye should come tae dinner with me, Duana."

Her chin lifted just a fraction of an inch, yet somehow, she gave him the impression she was looking down at him from her smaller height. "Why would I want to do that?" she asked.

"Because I'm hungry," he said. "And I dinna want tae eat alone."

She gave him a strange look, and he couldn't blame her. His words had held a strange honesty that rang painfully true, even to his own ears. He often ate on his own, despite the fact he was the alpha of a large group of wolves. For being alpha also put him outside of the pack in many ways, and Cedric found he was often alone, much more so than he would like to be. But he wouldn't go begging to be invited. Och, no. For that would show weakness, and would only be inviting others to challenge his position.

And besides, the wolves closest to him were all mated now. He would just be a…what was the saying…a third wheel.

"You should go with him, Princess," Prince Nada insisted gently.

Och, now the daft prince was feeling sorry for him, too? With all eyes on him, Cedric smoothed back his hair and checked the band holding his low ponytail.

"No, I should not," Duana responded.

The prince's smile slipped from his face as he turned to study his daughter. "Oh, but I insist," he told her in no uncertain terms.

Her expression hardened, her wee features tightening until it appeared to be made of stone as she stared back.

Cedric waited, wondering what her decision would be. He knew the prince didn't intimidate her. At least not as much as he should. It was one of the things he liked about her. Of course, now that he knew who the prince truly was to her, he understood why.

"Fine," she said after a long pause. "I'll go. But only to get the hell away from you." With that she stomped down the hall to her bedroom, or what he assumed was her bedroom.

"Excellent!" The prince clapped his hands together, the exaggerated smile Cedric knew better than to trust returning to his face.

He turned that smile to Cedric. It gave him the creeps, but he managed to return a bit of the prince's happiness to him.

"I knew she would come to her senses. It's that *an olc* blood in her, you know."

Once he heard her door shut, Cedric looked down at the prince. His royal pain in the arse was quite tall, but still shorter than Cedric's six foot seven inches. "I decided tae take ye up on yer deal," he told him. "I will court the princess, and try tae get her mind off o' saving the ones who can no' be saved." He was very careful not to say the word "mate". "And by doing so,

17

perhaps we can keep her out of our hair, and maybe I can even change her mind over time."

"Yes," the prince agreed. "You can distract her with sex."

Cedric nearly choked on his own spittle. The thought had crossed his mind one or five hundred times, aye, but it wasn't something he would say aloud. Especially not to this one, who already knew too much as it was. "I will do my best to keep her distracted," he said.

He was saved from hearing anymore when Duana came back into the room. Her hair was still on top of her head, and she hadn't changed her clothes at all, other than to put on a pair of slip-on sneakers.

"Is that what you're wearing?" the prince asked her. The disapproval in his voice was impossible to miss.

A sudden rush of anger filled Cedric, but before he could come to her defense, Duana's chin rose. "Yes," she told him shortly, the look in her eyes daring him to say anything else about it.

"It's fine," Cedric said. "We're no' going anywhere fancy."

"See?" she told the prince. Turning on her heel, she went over to a closet he hadn't noticed before and pulled out a light jacket. As she passed Cedric on her way out of the house, she didn't even give him so much as a glance.

With a nod to the prince, he followed her out of the little house.

Outside, she stopped. "Where's your car," she said. It was not spoken as a question, more as an accusation.

"It's in the shop," he told her as he ran an appreciative eye over his new 2020 Midnight Blue Harley Davidson Fat Boy 114 motorcycle. "Getting some work done. So, we'll have tae take this."

"So you can risk my life," she said with no emotion.

"There's no risk involved, lass. It would take more than a little motorcycle accident tae kill ye." He saw her head tilt to the side as she took in the V-Twin engine and Lakester disc wheels. "Am I wrong?"

She glanced at him out of the corner of her eye. "You're not wrong," she said. "But that doesn't mean I want to be scraped along the road like cheese on a grater. I just bought these pants."

"Dinna fash yerself," he told her. "I will no' let that happen. I even have an extra helmet." Unzipping a leather saddlebag, he pulled out a black helmet.

"I'm so glad I didn't waste time doing my hair," she said, taking the helmet from him. "What about you?"

He narrowed his eyes in amusement at the sarcasm dripped from her voice. "Me?"

"Where's your helmet?"

"I dinna need one," he informed her.

"Correct me if I'm wrong," she told him. "But isn't it a law that you have to wear a helmet in this state?"

"Och." He waved a hand in the air, dismissing silly things such as rules and laws. Although it was true. "For humans."

"By the way, in case I wasn't completely clear. I'm only doing this to get away from that one." She pointed a thumb over her shoulder toward the house they'd just left. "He's driving me completely insane."

"I can see how it would be easy for that tae happen."

"This does not mean we're friends," she told him.

"O' course not," Cedric responded with all seriousness. "It would take more than a cheap meal tae make friend o' you, I ken."

Colors flared within her eyes as she glanced at him, only briefly, as she tried to decide if he was making fun of her. Then, with a sigh reeking of resignation, she stuck the helmet on her head. "Well, let's go, wolf," she told him. "I am actually hungry. And my temperament does not get any better if you make me wait."

Checking his ponytail again, even though he'd already done so when he'd arrived, Cedric threw one leg over the monster bike and pushed the starter. Putting up the kickstand, he easily held the weight of the bike steady as Duana climbed onto the back, her soft curves settling in behind him like she belonged there. A low growl vibrated deep within his chest, and he hoped she wouldn't be able to hear it over the roar of the engine.

Her arms came around his waist and she linked her fingers low on his stomach, right about at belt level.

Cedric took a shuddering breath, put the bike into gear, and pulled away from driveway.

The twenty minutes it took to get to the restaurant were the longest twenty minutes he'd ever experienced in his life. And when he finally pulled into a parking slot, he released a breath he didn't realize he'd been holding, because he didn't think he could stand her wrapped around him another minute.

Every time he'd hit the slightest bump in the road her arms had tightened around his waist, her breasts rubbing along his back as the insides of her soft thighs hugged his hips tighter.

The bike had seemed a great idea when he'd thought of it, but now...

Well, now, he wasn't so sure he'd make it through the night without suffering from a serious case of blue balls.

CHAPTER 3

Duana watched the alpha wolf sitting across from her as he folded his menu and gave it back to the waitress, and it took everything she had not to run screaming from the room.

But not for the reasons she should.

The restaurant wasn't large, but it was homey, even with its high ceilings and spacious seating. The table they sat at was built well, with a square, oak top and sturdy legs, yet the wolf's large frame dwarfed the thick wood. His muscular chest and shoulders hid the chair he sat on. And his biceps, when he crossed his forearms on the edge of the table, bulged until she was certain the cotton seams of his black T-shirt were about to tear. His forearms and hands were strong, his waist lean and ribbed with muscle, as was the rest of his body.

She knew this because sitting behind him on the motor-cycle was like being wrapped around one of those marble statues come to life, delightfully warm and able to move on its own.

He could crush her with one hand.

Her thighs clenched as the ache between them grew.

But when she raised her gaze to his, his expression was open and friendly as his eerie eyes traveled over her face. This contradiction was not something she was not used to in her world. Duana wasn't sure how to react to it.

So, she stared.

Swallowing hard, she tore her eyes from his striking jaw and looked around as she tried to get her raging libido under control. At least he'd brought her to a good restaurant. It was family owned and local. And they served good homemade meals, like meat and potatoes. Something that would fill a girl up.

As long moments went by, the silence began to peck at her. Duana peeked up at him from underneath her lashes. "So, Cedric. What is this about?"

He took a long drink of his Guinness and leveled that steady stare upon her. Other than a few words about how he'd eaten there before and how good the food was, he'd said nothing since they'd arrived except to order his meal. But now she needed answers.

"Well," he said. "I could tell ye a tale, but that would no' get us anywhere. So, I think honesty will do us better."

"Please," she said. "I always prefer the truth over games."

He set his beer down on the table and leaned back in his chair. "The prince thinks I should mate with ye."

Duana sat back, crossing her arms over her chest to keep her heart from beating right out of it. To keep him from noticing, she kept talking. "Really?" she asked.

"Aye, 'really'," he told her.

"What in the world makes him think that I would want to mate a mangy dog like you."

It wasn't meant as a question, and he didn't take it as one. His eerie white-blue eyes narrowed in on her face. "Ye did no' think I was so mangy the first time we met."

She didn't think so now, either. But that was neither here nor there. "I'm sure I don't know what you mean," she told him.

"Aye, but I think ye do," he said. "I saw how the colors flashed in yer eyes when ye were standing so close tae me."

His arrogance truly knew no bounds. "My eyes do that when I'm angry," she informed him. "As a matter of fact, they're about to do it right now. In front of all of these nice, innocent humans."

His own eyes flashed white, even though there was no one sitting near enough to them to hear what she'd said.

Well, well. Wasn't this interesting? "Don't tell me that you care about these people," she drawled.

"As a matter o' fact, I do," he said in a low voice. "I have some good friends who are human. Or, at least, human enough."

"What's that supposed to mean?" she asked.

"They're witches," he said quietly. "As I said, human enough."

A hot light of pain pierced her gut at his words, and it took her a moment to identify it for what it was—envy. Exactly how many witches did he know? And what kind of spells did they cast on him in the dark of the night?

Duana shook off such inappropriate, and completely uncalled for, thoughts. "What does that have to do with anything?" she asked. She sounded poised and calm to her own ears. Hopefully, her eyes were following suit.

"They're good people," he gritted out. "Just as I'm sure these people are good people. And I dinna want tae have tae kill them because ye can no' be discreet."

He was saved from her wicked tongue when the waitress showed up with their food, setting a large steak and mashed potatoes down in front of him in, and a slightly smaller steak and mashed potatoes down in front of her.

His chest rose and fell on a deep breath as he closed his eyes and inhaled the mouth-watering scent of his dinner. The waitress hovered awkwardly near the table, watching him, until he opened his eyes and noticed her there. With a smile, he thanked her and sent her on her way.

Duana watched with amusement as the young girl hesitated, shifting her weight back and forth awkwardly before she finally tore her eyes away from his imposing form. She appeared both horribly attracted to and terrified of the male sitting at her table. "This is fine," Duana told her, a little louder than was necessary. "Thank you," she added. After all, she wouldn't want the girl to spit in her wine.

The waitress flicked her eyes briefly in her direction and gave her a tight smile. "Just let me know if you need anything." Then she darted off toward the kitchens.

Picking up her knife and fork, Duana cut off a large piece of steak and put the entire thing in her mouth. It was cooked perfectly, and her eyes nearly rolled back in her head as she chewed the tender morsel. Swallowing, she took a sip of her merlot, then patted the corners of her mouth with her napkin.

Ah, this dinner was almost worth the company.

She was cutting off a second piece when she felt the wolf's

eyes on her. Sure enough, when she glanced up, he was sitting perfectly still, knife in one hand and fork in the other, and he was staring.

Duana lifted one eyebrow in question.

"I like a woman who can eat," he told her, approval deepening his voice.

"As if I care," she replied. Putting the bite in her mouth, she chewed slowly.

He narrowed his eyes. "If my company is so unbearable, kitten, why did ye agree tae come here then?"

Her heart stuttered at the nickname. "I already told you. I needed to get away from the prince. I couldn't stand being in that house another moment."

"There are other things ye could have done tae get away from him," he pointed out. "Ye could have taken a walk. Ye could have gone for a drive. Ye could have 'whooshed' away like ye Faeries do tae go wherever the hell ye want tae go."

She ground her teeth, a scathing rebuttal burning the tip of her tongue. But instead of responding, she squeezed her eyes closed for a moment and took a deep, calming breath before opening them again. She wasn't angry at him. She was angry at herself. Because the sad truth was, he was right. There were many other things she could have done. But she would continue to tell herself she'd only gone with him because he had been the first available option.

And because she was hungry.

And that was what she would tell anyone who asked. The only other option would be to admit to a truth even she, herself, was not ready to face.

Speaking of which, she asked, "So, what are we going to do about the prince's request? Because it's quite obvious that this"

—she gestured between the two of them with her fork— "will never work."

"Are ye so verra sure aboot that?"

"Oh, I am quite certain." She tried some of the mashed potatoes.

He shrugged and cut into his steak. "I'm no' so bad, ye know."

"No?"

"No. And I'm a fookin' great kisser," he told her. When he looked up, chewing his steak, his expression was dead serious. He swallowed and took a sip of his beer, and when he spoke again, his voice was so deep it was nearly a growl. "Ye'll never ken what yer missing out on if ye dinna give me a chance, kitten."

Heat pooled between her thighs, so hot she nearly gave herself away by squirming on her chair.

As it was, Duana's skin felt flushed, and she knew by the way he was staring the colors were flashing in her eyes. The wolf was only teasing, trying to get a reaction out of her. And, dammit, it was working. She knew this. She did.

Yet, before she could stop herself, her eyes dropped to his lips.

They were perfect lips. Masculine lips. Like the face surrounding them. Not too thin, not too thick, and meant to be kissed.

Or, to do the kissing.

Images flashed through her mind of those lips pressed to her skin, like broken reels of one of the human porn movies. Dropping soft kisses along her jaw, against the side of her neck. His long hair hanging loose, soft as silk against the hard tips of her breasts, sliding down her arm as he made his way lower...

Her tongue wet her bottom lip as she stared, halfway between her fantasies and her real life, at the male who was so close and yet so far away.

"Dinna stare at me like that, kitten. Ye'll be putting ideas in my head. And I dinna think yer ready for that. Yet."

Angry at him for his lack of discretion and even more angry at herself—for reasons she couldn't fathom—her fork fell from her fingers to land on the wooden tabletop with a clatter. Trying to regain her composure, she wiped her mouth with her napkin. "I need to go to the ladies room," she announced, shoving back her chair. She left the table with no idea where she was going, but felt his eyes burning into her back the entire way. Stopping at the bar, she got directions to the bathroom and headed swiftly in that direction.

Once she was behind the closed door, she felt some of the tightness ease in her chest. Sucking in a lungful of air, she collapsed against the wall.

This had been such a bad idea, coming here with him. Because no matter what she tried to tell herself, for some odd reason she was...attracted to him.

And, apparently, she really sucked at hiding it.

Walking over to the sink, she splashed cold water on her face and tried to get her rioting hormones under control. Lifting her head, she stared at the woman in the mirror. "Why do I put myself into these situations with him?"

But the woman staring back at her had no advice.

"This was a bad idea," she repeated out loud. Taking a deep breath, she washed her hands, dried off her face, and pushed her shoulders back. She would not be dissuaded from her meal by an overgrown puppy. She hadn't been lying when she'd said she was hungry. And the food here really was very good.

Besides, this was all his fault, upsetting her like this. He really needed to learn how to behave himself.

When she arrived back at the table, Cedric pushed his chair back and stood. The chivalrous act took her by surprise and she paused with one hand on the back of her chair, unsure of what to do. Were they leaving? But she still had food on her plate.

When he just stood there waiting, she finally realized he was only standing out of a misguided sense of manners from a time long ago. Duana sat down, her face flaming. Cedric also took his seat, picked up his knife and fork, and resumed eating like nothing at all had happened.

Duana followed suit.

"Are ye all right, lass?"

"I'm fine." Catching the eye of the waitress, she signaled for her to bring more wine.

Cedric waited for her wine to be poured before asking for another beer. When the waitress ran off to get it for him, Duana again found herself at the center of his focus. "So, kitten," he said. "Tell me, how is it that ye had the bad misfortune o' ending up with the prince?"

Duana took a sip of wine to stall for time, thinking of how she should answer him. If she refused to tell him anything, it would look entirely too suspicious. Much as she tried to cut him down, this wolf was not unintelligent.

She decided to follow his example and tell him the truth. At least up to a point, because surely, even if she was utterly convincing, he'd be able to smell a lie with that nose of his. "My brother brought me to the prince when I was young," she told him.

"After the war." He nodded. This was something he'd already known.

"Yes," she told him. "The rest of my family had acquired the addiction, and they were exiled into the vortex. Back to our world," she clarified when he lifted a brow at her choice of words. "My brother and I were the only Dark Fae left, or so we believed at the time. He brought me to the prince under a flag of truce hoping he would spare me, because I was young enough and well-traveled enough not to have any loyalties to one tribe or the other." She gave a small shrug. "And he did."

"How old were ye?"

"I was a woman grown, barely, but much younger and more naive than I am now." She tilted her wine glass, watching how the ruby liquid coated the sides of the glass. It was a good vintage. "Months later, I found out my brother had been killed by a wolf as he'd tried to escape back into our own dimension."

Cedric set down his fork and leaned back in his chair, his expression careful. "Why did yer brother not take ye with him back tae yer own world?" he asked after a pause.

"Because it was too dangerous there now. With no other way to get their fix, the addicted ones were sure to come after any of us who hadn't succumbed."

"And ye've been with him ever since? Prince Nada?"

She nodded, grateful for the question. She didn't like thinking about her older brother. "Yes. Although, for the last twenty years or so, I haven't been so inclined to keep his company. At least, not before I came here."

"Perhaps it's no' the faerie prince keeping yer attention."

Duana leveled him with a steady stare. "What else would it

be?" He opened his mouth to speak, but she cut him off. "My people are on the verge of inundating this world. Of course, I am going to be here. For good or bad. I am their princess. I will lead those I can."

He gave her a nod, his light eyes shining with something she couldn't quite read. "And those ye can't lead? The soul suckers?"

"I will do what needs to be done to save the sane remnants of my tribe."

"What was yer life like living with his royal pain in the arse?" The note of disgust in his voice was tempered by a layer of awe. "I dinna ken that I would have the patience."

"It was...interesting." She cleared her throat. "What about you?" she asked, needing to change the subject before he got too curious. "What was your life like as a young pup in the wilds of the Scottish Highlands?"

Cedric took a bite of potatoes, his eyes drifting off to the side in thought as he chewed. "I guess ye could say it was a normal upbringing. Whatever that's supposed tae mean. I was born in tae a good pack with two good parents where I was raised well and taken care o'."

"Why did you come to this country if things were so great over there?"

His eyes dropped down to his plate as he lifted one shoulder. "I dinna ken," he told her. "Change of scenery, perhaps."

Duana watched him closely. He was hiding something. "Are your parents still alive?"

"I dinna ken," he told her after a pause. "I have no' spoken tae them in quite a while. But I would assume so."

Pushing her plate aside, Duana rested her elbows on the

table and interlaced her fingers. Now things were getting interesting. "Did you have a falling out?"

His mouth pressed into a thin line. "If ye dinna mind, princess, I would prefer no' tae speak o' it."

She tilted her head and studied his expression. She would be getting no more information out of him tonight. "I'm sorry," she told him. "I didn't mean to pry."

"Aye, ye did," he said. "But I dinna mind. It's just a story for another time. Why ruin this fine meal speakin' o' such unpleasant things?"

Following his lead, she picked up her knife and fork, and they finished their meal in comfortable silence. It wasn't until the waitress set a plate of cheesecake in front of him that Cedric spoke again. "So, what are we tae do aboot this idea yer…prince has?"

Duana did not miss the catch in his question. "What do you mean?" she asked, then answered her own question. "There's nothing to do. Because it's not happening."

He licked cheesecake off his fork with a thoughtful look on his face. "I agree," he told her. "But perhaps we could make him think it is happening."

"Why would we do that? It would only anger him when he found out. And he would find out."

"Ye have tae ken he's crazy as a loon."

"I do," she told him. "But he's also the crazy loon who's going to free my people. As soon as I can figure out this cure."

"Och, Duana. Ye canna mean tae still be on that. I thought ye said ye would do what needs tae be done?"

"Of course, I am. If there is any way I can give them their lives back, I will. Wouldn't you want to help your own people if the tables were turned?"

"No," he answered in all seriousness. "I would put a bullet in their heads tae end their suffering."

"You can't mean that."

"But I do. There's no cure for them," he told her. "Ye ken this, lass. There's nothing ye can do."

"I disagree." She shook her head. "I'm close. I'm very close to finding a cure."

"Duana…"

"Cedric, please." She held up her hand, stopping whatever he was about to say. "This wasn't a friendly date at all, was it? The real reason you brought me here was to try to talk me out of healing my people." Her mouth twisted in disgust. "You're wasting your time. I've told you before, and I'll tell you again, I'm not stopping until I find a cure for them." She pointed at his chest. "And you promised that you would give me the time to do that."

"Aye. You're right. I did tell ye that," he told her. "And I will." He pointed his fork at her. "But dinna think for one moment I will allow ye tae put any o' us in danger. No' me, no' my pack, no' even yourself."

"I completely understand," she ground out. "Although you may not have any say in the matter. You are not one of my people. You are not my father or my king." Picking up her wine, she swallowed down the last of it and stood up from the table. "I believe it's time for me to go home."

Cedric frowned up at her. "Will ye no' let a man finish his dessert?"

"Go ahead," she told him. "I can walk." As she turned away, she paused. "Or maybe I'll just whoosh away to wherever I want to be." Turning on her heel, she stalked out of the restaurant. He tried to call her once, but she ignored him. Even when she heard the crash of dishes and the waitress calling out something about paying the bill, she didn't stop and look back, but just kept going.

She couldn't believe that she had come here with him. What the ever-loving hell had she been thinking? That he was her friend? Duana didn't have friends. She had subjects. Or she had enemies.

Hell, she didn't even like him.

She was out the door and walking down the sidewalk when he caught up to her.

Grabbing her by the upper arm, he pulled her to a halt. "Princess, wait. Wait!"

Yanking her arm from his grip, she spun around. "Let me go," she told him. "I don't know why I allowed you both to talk me into coming here with you. I had a frozen pizza I could've thrown in the oven."

His head lowered until their foreheads nearly touched. "Because ye were hungry enough, and no' just for food. And ye still are."

Despite the sexy growl of his voice that tightened the muscles deep in her core and made her catch her breath, Duana managed to roll her eyes in a show of indifference and turned to walk away. She couldn't control her body's reaction, but she would control her outward response.

He released a hard breath behind her. "Duana! Wait," he called. "I am sorry. I gave ye my word that I would give ye the chance tae help yer people, and I need tae keep it. I will take ye home if that's where ye want to go." He held out his hand.

Duana stared at it like it was a five-headed serpent. And as far as she was concerned, it was. Ready to strike her down and fill her with venomous thoughts and urges.

Rolling his eyes much as she had only moments before, only with much more drama, Cedric's head fell back on his neck and he spoke to the sky above them. "Give it a rest, princess. I am no' that bad, and ye know it." He leveled his gaze on her. "Och, come on, then." Taking her hand, he kept a firm grip on her as he led her back to the motorcycle, handed her the spare helmet, and got on. Raising the kickstand, he pressed the starter and the engine roared to life. Staring straight ahead, he waited.

Duana weighed the options of walking home or hitching a ride, and ultimately decided getting a ride would definitely be easier on her feet, if not her anxiety. So, she fastened the helmet on her head and climbed onto the back.

His hard body nestled between her thighs like he belonged there, and she caught a light whiff of something dark and spicy as the wind blew tendrils of his ponytail against her face. His hair was like silk against her lips. A shiver ran down her spine —from the wind and most definitely not the way he smelled— and she lowered the face shield. Taking a deep breath, she braced herself for the contact before she wrapped her arms around his waist.

Cedric turned his head to look for cars, and Duana was gifted with an up close and personal view of his handsome profile, only inches from hers.

She had the insane urge to kiss his hard jaw so she could feel the contrast of the roughness of his beard. Luckily, the helmet kept her from embarrassing herself.

The ride home was even longer than the ride to the restaurant, but once back at the prince's house, she climbed off the death mobile, took off her head protection, and handed it back to him. "Thank you for dinner. And for the ride," she told him automatically.

"Twas my distinct pleasure, lass." His tone was decidedly less robotic.

She stood awkwardly for a moment, both wanting to leave and wanting to stay, until finally, lowering her eyes, she turned abruptly on her heel and walked away.

Between one breath and the next, he was looming in front of her, blocking her path. He was so close she could smell the clean, woodsy scent of his skin. Duana hadn't even heard him turn off the motorcycle.

"I think yer forgetting something," he told her.

He was so close to her, she had to crank her head way back to look into his face. But she refused to retreat. It would only make the game of hunter and prey that much more fun for him. "And what is that?" she asked, not even trying to hide the sarcasm in her voice.

One side of his mouth lifted in a devilish smile as he slid his hand up the side of her throat, tilting her head back even more with his thumb beneath her chin. "This," he told her.

And then his lips found hers.

The kiss was barely a whisper of a touch at first, and Duana's breath caught, for the feeling was completely alien to her. Despite her upbringing, or perhaps because of it, she had always had those who were there to serve her, in any way she wished.

She'd been pleasured by both males and females in many an intimate manner. But Duana found it all exceedingly underwhelming, and eventually decided it was all nothing but a waste of time.

However, she'd never actually been kissed.

At his gentle urging, her lips parted, releasing the breath she'd been holding. He took that as encouragement and increased the pressure, drawing her bottom lip between his own, running his tongue along the seam of her mouth.

Tasting. Probing. He tasted dark, like the beer he'd had at dinner. And a little bit wild, like the creature he was.

With a low growl, his powerful arms slid around her body, pulling her up into him until her toes barely touched the ground and she could feel his heart pounding against her chest. She gasped at the heat of his body, every inch of her touching every hard inch of him.

Duana clung to his powerful shoulders, trying to ground herself, awash with an overpowering need that raced through her veins and centered between her legs until her womb felt heavy and wetness appeared between her thighs.

His large hand roamed over her back and down over the curve of her behind, squeezing her flesh as he plundered her mouth with his lips and tongue. Taking what he wanted without asking.

And it was very obvious by the hard length growing against her stomach that what he wanted was her.

Before she could stop herself, she groaned, feeling drunk on wine and werewolf. Her wordless plea was met by a roll of his hips against hers, his kisses roughened by a desperate need that was echoed within her.

With a nip on her bottom lip, he whispered against her mouth, "Tis only proper tae get a goodnight kiss after I take ye tae dinner." Then he pressed his lips hard against hers once more and released her.

Duana stumbled a bit before she caught herself. The air was cool against her where she had once been warm, cooling her passion. Before she could put together a coherent sentence to tell him that was an old-fashioned notion and she didn't owe him a damn thing, he was back on his motorcycle and pulling away.

Duana watched him leave, her chest heaving and her eyes lighting the night with colors.

CHAPTER 4

Cedric was still shaken up when he got back to his apartment. He sat on his bike for a minute with the engine off, listening to the breeze ruffle the trees and the nocturnal animals hunt for their dinner. Breathing deep, he waited until he'd calmed his ardor before he swung his leg over the seat and entered the building, the helmet the princess had worn tucked under his arm.

It smelled fresh and clean like her hair.

He'd hated leaving Duana there like that, but he'd been afraid if he didn't, he would've dropped to his knees and begged her to let him touch her, and with that simple act he would've shown her the power she held over him. Power he was only now beginning to understand.

Walking through the doorway, he wasn't surprised to see the Faerie prince sitting in his favorite chair, obviously waiting for him.

When he spotted Cedric, he jumped up, clapping his hands

together with excitement. "Well," he asked with an expectant expression. "How did it go?"

Cedric paused with his hand still on the doorknob. His eyes fell briefly to the helmet under his arm. "It went verra well," he told his very much expected guest. "Or, as well as expected with a lass such as Duana."

Clapping his hands together like an overexcited seal, the prince walked up to him, a new pep in his step that hadn't been there before. Taking Cedric's free hand within his own, he leaned in until the boundaries of personal space were nonexistent. "I knew you would come to your senses! And Duana will come around, don't you worry. I have no doubts at all."

Cedric pulled his hand out of the prince's clammy grip and set the helmet down on the counter. "Aye," he said. "I canna argue with the fact that she is a Bonnie lass. I could do much worse in my choice o' a mate."

He didn't bother to tell the prince how it wasn't really his choice to make, but the choice of his wolf. No matter how attracted he was to a lass, it was the beast inside of him who would pick the female who was best suited to it.

The prince stepped back and gave him a skeptical look. "You have something on your mind," he concluded.

"Aye, I do." Cedric walked over to the fridge. Opening the stainless steel door, he grabbed a beer, popped off the top, and took a long drink before turning his attention back to the Fae prince.

"What is it exactly that concerns you?" the prince asked. "You just said yourself how attracted you are to the princess."

"I just…I dinna ken if this plan is going to work."

Prince Nada appeared genuinely concerned. "Why would you think that?"

Cedric paused with the bottle of brew halfway to his mouth. "In case ye haven't noticed, the princess is a wee bit strong-willed."

"Yes," the prince agreed without hesitation. "And stubborn."

Cedric took another good swig of his beer in the hopes it would calm the beast within him, still prowling restlessly beneath his skin. It hadn't been happy to get back on the bike and come home. "And I dinna think she wants tae be mated tae me."

The prince waved a hand in the air as though what the princess wanted was inconsequential. "She'll come around. You're a very handsome male. You're strong. You're loyal. And it's quite obvious by the way she refuses to spend time with you that your presence anywhere near her sets off all of her feminine bells and whistles. Why wouldn't she want to be with someone like you?"

"Because she does no' love me," Cedric said. "She does no' even like me." And there it was, the crux of the matter. "And I dinna ken that she ever will. She thinks I am beneath her."

"Pfft. Nonsense!" Prince Nada dismissed his words like they were no more important to him than a mortal human's worry of such things. "Love is not important. As long as you can keep her occupied and content enough, she will be out of my hair."

Cedric felt a wave of anger rise up inside of him. "That's where yer wrong," he told him through gritted teeth. "Love is verra important. It's the most important thing other than trust, and she for sure does no' trust me."

The prince tilted his head to the side as a heavy weight seemed to settle over him, stilling his previous excitement. He leveled a chilling stare on Cedric, causing the hair to stand up on the back of his neck. "Well, then, you will just have to convince her otherwise." And on that parting order, he popped out of the room.

Cedric lifted the bottle of beer to his lips, never taking his eyes from the spot where the prince just stood, in case he changed his mind. His muscles shifted uneasily beneath his skin. He'd never get used to the way he did that.

He finished that beer and drank another one before he finally kicked off his boots and locked his front door, not that it would do him any good, and went to his room to change.

As he pulled off his shirt, Duana's cool, sweet scent filled his nose.

Snowdrops, he realized. She smelled like Snowdrops. The little, white bell flowers that grew all over Scotland. They had that same fresh scent...

And were just as poisonous to anyone who was foolish enough to taste them.

He suddenly felt her lips moving beneath his as memories of their kiss flooded his mind.

Och, aye, he was attracted to the lass and he knew she was attracted to him. Physically, at least. But what he had not expected was the explosion that had rocked him the moment his lips touched hers. Looking down, his cock strained against the front of his jeans, at the ready. "Easy there, boy," he told it. "There will no' be any o' that tonight."

It did not seem to believe him. He seriously thought about taking a cold shower to get her smell off of him, hoping that might dissuade his manly bits even further. But in the end, he just went out to the kitchen, got another beer, and sat in his favorite chair—the one the daft prince had just vacated. Picking up the remote, he pointed it at the TV. He was in the middle of watching the latest season of "Ozark," and it was just getting good.

But he never turned it on. Instead, his thoughts drifted back to his dinner with Duana. When he'd spoken to the others about this plan, it had seemed like a fine idea. A way to keep the prince happy and keep an eye on the *an olc* princess and her endeavors to save her kind.

However, now he wasn't so sure. His wolf bared its teeth, growling low. It thought this was a fine plan, indeed, and that was what truly worried him. Mating with a Faerie princess was not in his long-term life plan. This thing he was doing was only supposed to be an act. Not for the long term, or for any term, as a matter of fact. When he'd first rolled the idea around in his head, he'd truly believed it would work.

Och, aye. There was no way in hell he would go through with it. No matter how bonnie she was or what his wolf was trying to tell him. The thing was as daft as the Faerie prince.

Tossing the remote onto the table, he leaned forward and braced his elbows on his knees, letting his head hang loose on his neck. His ponytail tickled his arm as it slid over his shoulder.

Who was he trying to fool?

Cedric picked up his cell phone, unlocked the screen and typed in a message. Less than two minutes later, there was a response. Hauling himself out of his chair, he put his boots back on and left the apartment, locking it behind him.

Fifteen minutes later, he was waiting in the woods about a mile behind the apartments.

The moment Marc saw him, the smile of greeting fell from his face. "Is everything all right?" he asked. "Did something happen? Did something go wrong?"

Cedric held his hand up to stop his line of questions. "No, no," he said. "Everything is just fine. It all went according tae plan."

Marc visibly relaxed. "Duana liked her date, then?" he asked.

"To be honest, I dinna ken," Cedric admitted.

"Do ye think she'd be receptive tae another one?" Marc asked.

Cedric shrugged. "I'll go by again tomorrow. I was thinking o' taking her on a picnic."

Marc pressed his lips together into a tight line, but his eyes twinkled with amusement, giving him away.

Cedric rested his hands low on his hips. "Wha'?"

"A picnic, ye say?"

"Aye, a picnic. Females like picnics. Hell, I might even bring some champagne and strawberries."

Without so much as a smirk, Marc told him, "Well, if she does no' appreciate ye after that, let me know. I'll go on th' damn picnic with ye."

"If th' day ends th' same way as it did tonight, I may take ye up on it." He gave a meaningful look to the front of his jeans.

Marc barked out a laugh, and Cedric joined in. It felt good to laugh, a release of the tension that had been winding him up since the first time Prince Nada had "whooshed" him into his kitchen what seemed like forever ago. Wiping tears from his eyes, he felt Marc's gaze upon him once more. "Wha'?" he asked again. "Why do ye keep eyeing me like a lost puppy?"

"Because I think there's more tae this than what yer telling me."

Cedric linked his hands behind his neck and stared up at

the night sky. The stars were bright, making their summer appearance. He hardly ever saw them over the Winter Solstice.

"Ye ken ye can talk tae me, Cedric. I ken yer my alpha, but yer also my friend. And other than Duncan, I've been with ye the longest. Ye ken ye can trust me."

"Aye, I ken that." Cedric ran his hands over his ponytail, smoothing back hair that was perfectly fine to begin with. "I dinna ken that this is such a good idea, tae be honest."

"Wha'? Meeting in the woods for a run?" Marc looked around. "Tis safe enough with all o' the patrols ye have runnin' through the area."

"No," Cedric said. "No' that. Courting th' princess."

"But it was yer idea," Marc told him. "And personally, I think it's a verra good idea."

"I ken it was my idea," Cedric fought to keep his voice level. It wasn't Marc's fault he was off his head. "But tha' was before…" His words trailed off, unable to put what he was feeling into something that made sense.

Marc gave him a grave look. "Before what?"

Cedric clenched his jaw. He would not be sharing any intimate details of what had happened between him and Duana.

"Cedric. Before what?" Marc asked him again. "I thought ye said the date went great?"

"It did," Cedric responded. "And it did no'. And tha's the problem."

Marc stared at him, puzzled, before understanding donned over his expression. "Yer hot and bothered for the Faerie princess!"

"Och. Ye dinna ken the half o' it," Cedric told him. Clasping his hands behind his back, he began to pace back and forth, unable to stand still. Restless energy made his muscles twitch.

"I'm no' denying the fact I'm attracted tae the lass. O' course I am. Who wouldn't be?"

"I'm no'."

"Yer mated," Cedric told him. "Ye dinna see anyone but for yer Bronaugh, as it should be. She is th' missing part o' yer soul. But I…" He stopped, sighed, and lifted his gaze to his friend's. "I've never had someone like that. And I never truly missed it. But ever since I first saw tha' female, I'm longing for things I ne'er thought I would long for."

"But Duana, truly? I mean, no offense, Cedric, but she's kind o' a bitch."

"Aye, she is." He grinned. "That's one o' the things I like aboot her. She challenges me. Keeps me on my toes. She does no' fall at my feet like shifter females, most o' whom are only looking for protection, and no' someone they can truly care aboot and spend their life with."

"Ye think the princess can give you this?" Marc asked.

Cedric gave that the consideration it deserved. After a moment, he turned to look at him. "No," he admitted. "No, I dinna. But it's what I truly want from her." The truth had burst from him on a rush of breath. A truth he could barely admit to himself. "And yer the only one I can talk tae aboot this. I ken ye will understand." He was one of the few who would, his own lass being of the dark Fae.

Marc did not give him any pitying looks or sympathize with him in any way. He just nodded his head in understanding. And Cedric appreciated that.

After a long silence as they both got lost in their own thoughts, Marc took off his shirt and hung it up on the branch nearest him. "So, shall we go for that run? Do some hunting?"

"Aye. It's exactly what I need."

"Let me just text Bronaugh and let her know I'll be gone for a few hours."

"How is the lass, by the way?" Cedric asked.

Marc began to shrug off his question as he put his phone back in the pocket of his jeans, but stopped. "She's struggling," he said. "And I'm no' sure exactly why. She refuses tae talk tae me."

Cedric eyed the bruises on Marc's back as he turned around to take off his pants. "Did she do that tae ye?" he asked, trying to keep his tone even.

Naked, Marc turned around. "It's no' what ye think, Cedric. She has the darkness inside o' her, and it's tryin' tae claw its way free. I forced her tae take it out on me. It helps." A sly grin grew on his face. "She takes it out on me in the verra best o' ways. All that pent up energy." He shrugged. "The bruises and biting…she can no' hurt me very badly. So, I dinna mind, even though she feels awful aboot it. No matter how much I tell her no' tae."

"So," Cedric said. "In this instance, she's doing okay?"

"So far," Marc said.

"Just be sure tae let me know if things get worse." Laying his palm on Marc's bare shoulder, he waited until he met his eyes. "We will no' harm her," he told him. "Ye ken that. No' unless we absolutely have tae and it's the verra last resort. If we have tae, we'll lock her in a cage where she can no' hurt anyone, including ye, until we can fix it."

Marc nodded. "Thank ye. I truly appreciate tha'. But ye ken ye will have tae get through me before ye put my Bronaugh in a cage."

"O' course," Cedric told him with a grin. Then he sighed. "But, if by some miracle things work out with me and the

47

princess, I expect ye tae do the same for me." With a wink, he shucked off his clothes and hung them on the branch beside Marcs. "Let's go, then," he said. "I need this more than ye ken. It'll clear my head."

The sounds of bone popping and muscle tearing filled the forest, but neither wolf uttered a sound as the change overtook them. Once in their wolf forms, the brown wolf looked at the large black wolf beside him.

With a toss of his head, the black wolf howled to the rising moon, and led the hunt.

CHAPTER 5

Duana was just getting out the shower the next day when the prince suddenly appeared in the bathroom with her. Although she should be used to his lack of decorum by now, she still jumped near out of her skin.

Grabbing the towel from the rack, she quickly wrapped it around her nude form. Unlike the shifters her father had taken to hanging around with the last fifty years or so, she did not make a habit out of running around naked in front of others. "What do I tell you about popping into private places?" she snarled.

To his credit, his dancing eyes never dropped from her face. Strange as he was, and despite the fact she'd never felt close to him as a daughter should, Duana had never feared for her physical safety while under his care.

Mentally…well, that was another story.

He clapped his hands together. "You need to get ready. Get ready now!"

"What are you talking about?" She stepped carefully out of the old, white tub.

"The alpha wolf is here to take you on your date!"

"What?" He'd finally lost his mind completely. That was really the only explanation. "What date? We do not have a date. You're hallucinating."

"But of course you do. Why else would he be waiting for you in the other room?"

"The alpha is here," she stated deadpan. "In this house. Again." The notion was so ridiculous Duana couldn't hide her tone of disbelief. Other than the kiss he'd stolen at the end of the evening, Duana had done nothing to encourage the wolf or convince him she would seek out his company.

"This is what I'm telling you." Prince Nada grinned like the complete lunatic he was. "It's not good to make him wait too long. You'll never win him over that way. Wolves run hotter than other males, you know. They don't have the patience your other suiters had."

"What other suiters?" She waved the question away before he could give her an answer, one that was sure to be just as outlandish as the thought of her having a male after her. Males ran from her. "It's impossible the wolf is here," she said. "I told him last night I would not be seeing him anymore."

From the other room, a deep voice shouted, "No, it's no', because I am, in fact, here."

The prince giggled like a schoolgirl, and Duana rolled her eyes. If he were not quite so old, she was sure he would be jumping up and down with excitement.

The princess pulled the towel more securely around her and pushed the prince aside. "This is a one-person powder room," she ground out. Of course, if he would've found them a bigger house with a decent sized bathroom—or, even better, he respected her privacy at all—they wouldn't have this problem. Picking up a comb, she began to untangle her long hair. "Another 'date' is not happening," she said quite clearly to both males. She didn't bother to raise her voice. Obviously, the wolf could hear her and was not above eavesdropping. "I have things to do today."

Behind her, the prince caught her eyes in the mirror. They were no longer dancing. Angry colors flashed within them: a warning. "You will be going," he said. "You need to go. It's good for you to get out of the house."

Duana wanted so badly to tell him to shove it where the sun didn't shine, crude as that saying was. But she knew her place here was fragile, and she wasn't in any position to endanger that place. At least, not yet. Forcing a smile, she said, "Of course, I will. As soon as you get out of the bathroom and let me get dressed."

Joy once again plastered itself all over the prince's face, the change so complete it was hard to imagine him being any other way. "Oh good! I'll pop out and tell him you'll be ready momentarily." He disappeared as quickly as he'd appeared.

Duana stared at the spot he'd just vacated, wishing she could pop away just as easily to another place, another time. Hell, another world.

But there was only one other place she could go. And if she went there, she couldn't say for certain her father would allow her to come back.

With a sigh of resignation, she finished drying off and took her time getting ready, coating her skin with a sweet smelling lotion and drying every single strand of her hair. She even added a little makeup just to drag things out a bit.

In her room, dressed in nothing more than her lacy white underthings, she glanced out the window to see if the sun was shining. Pressing her hand against the glass, she felt the heat of the day rising, so she decided to dress lightly. Pulling out a sundress, she held it up in front of herself and went over to the mirror. It was pale yellow, not too flouncy, and came to about mid-thigh.

Remembering his hand on her behind the night before, and considering the ease of access the dress would provide, Duana had second thoughts. She put it back in the closet and pulled out some soft, creamy linen pants instead. Still light and airy, but covering more skin. She added a short sleeved, pale lavender, button down shirt, and slipped low-heeled sandals onto her feet.

It had been at least forty-five minutes since the wolf had shown up. She hoped he had lost patience and left, but that was not to be the case. For when she finally left her room, he was still there, sitting patiently on one end of the single couch while the prince fluttered about in the kitchen.

When the alpha wolf saw her, he unfolded his tall frame and got to his feet, his icy blue eyes flashing white lightning as they roamed over her body, lingering at her hips and chest before finally meeting her eyes. He gave her a possessive smile, and his voice was little more than a deep growl when he told her, "Ye look...bonnie is no' the word. Ye look stunning, princess. Sweet as the summer breeze."

Duana couldn't say the same for him. The alpha wolf was a menacing figure in black, except for the white-hot fire crackling in his eyes.

"I thought ye would like tae go for a picnic," he said. "Tis a beautiful day." The lightness of his words belied the intensity of his tone.

"You can't just keep showing up at my door, expecting me to drop everything else in my life to run off on...on...dates with you. I have things to do today. I don't have time for a picnic." Her lips twisted the word into something ugly, contradicting the picture she had in her head. Duana couldn't remember the last time she'd done something so simple as sit outside and eat food just to enjoy the pleasure of nature.

"I can help ye do those things if ye'd like," he told her. "After we eat, o' course." He pointed to the picnic basket at his feet.

She blinked, positive her eyes were deceiving her. "You even put it in an actual basket," she said.

"O' course," he said. "What's a picnic without a basket?"

Duana wondered what innocent girl the big, bad wolf had stolen it from.

The prince came out of the kitchen, a pink, ruffled apron tied around his waist over his expensive suit, drying his hands on a dish towel. "Go on kids," he told them. "Have fun, and don't worry about having her home at any particular time. She can stay out as late as she wants."

Cedric raised an eyebrow, and Duana turned to give the prince a dirty look, but didn't bother wasting her energy with a response to that parental silliness.

"After you, princess," Cedric told her, indicating the way to the door.

Duana inhaled, releasing the breath through her teeth. It appeared she was going on a picnic. "Do I need to bring money or a jacket?" she asked, her tone sugary sweet.

Cedric reared back, offended. "O' course no'." He shook his head to emphasize his answer, and his long, black ponytail swung against his back. "There's no need. I will take care o' ye, Duana."

She didn't know if it was the words he'd spoken or the ride or die way he'd said them, but despite her outward attitude, Duana's breath caught and her stomach twisted in knots.

No, she told herself. It wasn't what he'd said, it was the idea of spending any part of her day in the company of this particular wolf—again— that had brought about this vile reaction.

Lowering her eyes so he wouldn't see the longing in them, she proceeded him out the door.

Once they got outside, she was relieved to see he had brought his car-truck thing and she wouldn't be expected to risk her life, and her composure, on the back that motorcycle again.

"Well, I couldn't verra well balance a picnic basket on my motorcycle," he answered her thoughts without her having to speak them.

"What is this called again?" she asked.

"This beauty is an *El Camino*," he said with pride.

Like the alpha wolf, his vehicle was dark and sleek and powerful. And also a little bit old fashioned. But nonetheless, Duana was grateful to climb into the seat and have some good ol' steel barricading her in.

Cedric put the basket in the seat between them, then climbed in beside her.

Her stomach growled as the scent of something warm and fried filled the small space. Glancing over at the basket with undisguised longing, she saw the wolf was, indeed, prepared. A black, soft-looking jacket was folded on the center of the seat on top of a thick, padded quilt made of blue squares with a stitched design. The basket balanced on top of the pile.

Duana faced the front again as the car rumbled to life and Cedric pulled away from the house. She wondered if the coat smelled like him.

He made his way onto the highway before asking, "So, what is it ye needed tae do today?"

"Nothing you need to worry about," she told him.

He gave her a sideways glance. "I meant what I said, princess. I would be more than happy tae help ye."

"Don't you have wolfy things to do today?" she asked. "Territory to protect? Pissing contests to have?" The last thing she needed was him hanging around as she checked in on her test subjects, the weight of his disapproval like a noose around her neck.

"Aye, I do have things," he said with a grin. "But they can wait."

"Well, they must not be very important things," she told him.

"No' more important than ye, no." He glanced at her again out of the corner of his eyes.

Her face heated as she felt his gaze linger, traveling over her profile, but she refused to respond. There was no way he could actually mean what he'd just said. Why would he? She'd been nothing but a bitch to him since they'd met. It was the way it had to be. They were not friends. They could never be friends. He was only doing this to appease the prince. For what reasons, she couldn't fathom. But it surely had very little to do with her.

They rode in silence for another 10 minutes or so before she realized he was heading north of the city. A surge of panic swelled within her. "Where are we going? Tell me," she demanded when he didn't immediately respond.

But she didn't need him to say it out loud, knowing damn well this was the way to his den. Duana found the buckle for her seatbelt as she prepared to jump out of the vehicle. At the speed they were traveling, it was doubtful she'd be able to walk away without some injuries, but she didn't see that she had any other choice. There was no way she'd be able to take them all on. Not on her own. She would go invisible as soon as she stopped rolling, then run across the highway and into the trees. By the time he shifted to find her, she would be gone.

Cedric frowned at her in confusion. "I told you. We're going on a picnic."

"I didn't realize I was to be the main course." The words were little more than a hiss between her teeth.

"What are ye speaking o', lass?" Sudden understanding dawned across his face. "Och, no. I'm no' taking ye home tae feed my wolves," he said. "I just ken a good place up here. It's quiet and private. No' like the parks in the city, with people stepping on yer lunch as they walk over ye," he said.

Having said his peace, he turned east on 405 and headed into the mountains, and Duana eased her hand back onto her lap. A few minutes later, he pulled off the highway to a feeder road that ran alongside of it. In the side mirror, she watched as a cloud of dirt kicked up from the tires, following them like a shroud until the road came to a dead end, spilling into a wide empty, dirt lot.

Parking in a spot near a large wooden sign announcing the start of a trail, he got out and jogged around to her side to open the door before she could do it herself. For such a large male, he moved with grace and a coiled energy that seemed forever on the verge of exploding.

"Thank you," she told him as he helped her out of the car. After all, she wasn't completely without manners.

"Yer verra welcome, princess." Shutting her door, he opened the back and got out the picnic basket and the blanket before closing things up and locking it.

He took her hand as they entered the trail, and the movement was so natural Duana wondered if she even would've noticed, were it not for the bolts of electricity that shot straight from his palm to her nether regions.

Sucking in a quick breath, she barely refrained from yanking her hand from his grip. As it was, his fingers tightened around hers the moment contact was made, so pulling away now would not be able to be done gracefully. Rather than make a big deal out of it, and therefore alerting him to how his touch affected her, Duana let him assist her along the rocky trail.

Less than a quarter mile away from the lot, a clearing was carved out in the middle of the giant evergreens. Big enough to see any curious animals or other threats that might invade their lunch, and small enough to provide some shade and allow the sun to dapple through the trees, it appeared out of a fairytale, complete with bunches of wildflowers that resembled little, white bells on a tall stem alongside tiny, pink flowers.

Cedric paused upon entering the clearing, lifting his nose and sniffing the air. A look of satisfaction settled across his features, and he laid down the blanket, spreading it out in the grass and setting the basket down on top of it.

Duana tried not to stare at his lean, powerful thighs as he squatted down to fix one of the corners. As though he sensed her eyes on him, he caught her eyes and winked before straightening to his full height. Wandering away a bit, he smoothed back his hair as he searched the ground. Every so often he would stop and pick up a rock. When he had four, he brought them over to the blanket and secured the corners.

Kneeling on the edge, Cedric set the picnic basket down on the blanket and opened the top.

Feeling awkward and useless, Duana picked a spot as far away from him as she could possibly get, perching her butt on the opposite edge of the blanket with her sandaled feet in the grass. She watched in amazement as he began to pull out their lunch.

First, there was a bucket, already full of ice. Next, a bottle of some type of sparkling wine that he set in the ice to chill. After that was done, he laid a hunk of cheese and a loaf of crusty bread beside it. Digging around, he found a knife and set it beside the cheese.

The fried, greasy smell she'd gotten a whiff of in the car was solved when he pulled out a paper bag containing fried chicken legs. Following that was some sliced ham, a container of strawberries, watermelon cut into bite sized pieces, crackers, and what looked like some kind of spinach dip.

To her amazement, he still wasn't done. Digging around in the basket, he found an assortment of pickles. Last, but not least, a couple of Hershey's chocolate bars. How he'd fit it all in the basket, she had no idea.

Duana took a moment to look over the food with a practiced eye before she gave him a sideways glance. "Did you bring anything for yourself to eat?"

At her unexpected teasing, his eyes clashed with hers in surprise. The corners of his mouth twitched, slowly widening into a playful smile that was even more devastating than his predatory one. "Ye can eat first," he offered. "I'll take what's left.

However, we may have tae stop somewhere for dessert on the way home."

On the way home. He made it sound like they'd be going there together, to a place they shared.

An image flickered through Duana's head of Cedric's apartment, only this time with her things lying around as well.

"What's wrong, kitten?"

Duana blinked a few times, and the image blew away on the breeze. Giving him a tight smile, she said, "I was kidding." Mostly.

He pulled out a few paper plates. "Ye eat as much as ye want," he told her. "I was serious about the dessert."

She was surprised to find herself smiling.

"May I?" he asked, indicating the food and the plate.

"Please," she said. She watched as he carefully chose the best pieces for her, setting the plate down by her hip before serving himself.

Silence reigned for a few minutes as they dug into their food. The chicken was cooling fast, but still delicious. The fruit perfectly ripe and sweet. The bread warm from sitting in the basket beside the drumsticks. Duana took her time eating, enjoying the trills of the birds and the rustling of the trees as the warm breeze blew through the branches.

Cedric's plate was empty in record time. As he watched her, a thoughtful expression came over his face. "So tell me princess, why do ye stay with him?"

The bread and cheese melted in her mouth and she smiled. "Who?" she asked, her mind still on the food.

"The daft prince," he said.

She took a moment to think about that. Why did she stay?

But the answer, when it came, was simple and honest. "Because I have nowhere else to go," she told him.

"Surely that canna be true," he said. "What of yer people? We ken now there's more o' yer kind who escaped the war than we first estimated. I've met some of them."

"There are," she said. "And they're hunted by your kind still, though they make no trouble—"

"Unless they're trying to suck out your soul," he chimed in.

The princess set down her plate, having suddenly lost her appetite. "Just say it," she said. "Say you don't think I can help them."

"I did no' say that," he told her.

"But it's what you're thinking. And you've said it before."

Leaning back on his hands, he stretched his long legs out in front of him, crossing his feet at the ankles. "I think it's highly unlikely," he told her. "I have another question for ye, though. Which is, what will happen? What will ye do when ye discover that they canna be cured?"

There was only one answer to that question. "Then we're all doomed," she admitted. "They will feed more viciously than any vampire until there is nothing left. They will take over the world."

Her answer was sobering, and something she had not wanted to admit to herself until just now. But really, what choice did she have? The soul suckers would get out. And the only way to save not only her own *an olc* tribe but the *na maithe*, the shifters, the vampires, even the humans and every other species was to cure them before they could succumb to their addiction.

"They dinna have tae get out, ye ken?" he told her. "We can keep them where they are."

She gave him a sharp look, but he held up his hand to stop her before she could speak. "No' tae kill them," he told her. "We can capture the ones who are out now and hold them until ye can try yer cure."

"And if it doesn't work?" Duana had never spoken these words aloud until now. Her head felt light as she admitted her greatest fear.

"Then we can send them back tae their own world. And this time we can seal it."

"That's impossible." She shook her head. "The portal is widening every moment, and soon all will understand how to breach it."

"We have Keelin," he told her. "She is The Key."

Duana shook her head, her brief pleasure in the day gone. "If only it were that easy. She is The Key, yes. But she's not the only one needed to close the portal. What we need...it takes great faerie magic."

"Well then, we will do what it takes."

"Why are you doing this?" she asked. "Really?"

"Doing what, princess?"

"Continuing this charade of courting me. Is it just to make the prince happy?" She held her breath as she waited for his answer, not knowing until now how much his answer meant to her.

He uncrossed his ankles and pulled his knees up, wrapping his arms around them as he gave her a contemplative look. "Once again," he said. "I believe honesty will be the best policy here. I could tell ye a tale, but ye probably would no' believe me. And, anyway, I dinna want tae lie tae ye."

"Why not?"

"Because trust is a verra important thing." His eerie eyes

never left her face. "And I do no' want tae break my trust with ye. So I will tell ye the honest answer to your question." He paused. "I'll admit, when Prince Nada first came tae me with this idea, I thought he was off his rocker and there was no way in hell I would agree tae it."

Pain flared in her chest. "You can stop there," she told him. "I don't need to know anymore."

"Aye, ye do," he told her. "For that's no' the whole answer. As I was saying before I was so rudely interrupted..." He gave her a wink. "I told the prince he was crazy and there was no way I was going tae do that. But I can no' lie tae myself and say that I'm no' attracted to you. Because I am. Verra much so. And so then I thought, 'Why no'? Why no' see?'"

"That's your answer." She arched one eyebrow. "I think she's hot, so why not?"

His expression settled into serious lines. "I like ye, kitten. Despite yer crazy ideas, ye light a fire in my blood that no one has ever done before. And no' just with yer face and yer body—though both are the bonniest I have ever seen—but with yer sharp wit and tongue." His eyes flared with white heat. "And yer passion. I find that I like it verra much," he told her. "I like how I feel when I'm around ye, even when yer tearing me down."

Tears pricked behind her eyes. Though not eloquent, his admission was honest and true, and one of the nicest things any male had ever said to her. Swallowing hard, she tried to regain her composure. "So...what? You're just going to keep showing up at my door every day expecting me to drop everything to come with you so you can 'date me'?" She made air quotes with her fingers.

"Well, if I had yer number I would call beforehand and make plans."

"I don't have a phone," she said.

"Ye dinna have a phone?"

She shook her head. "I have no need. We fairies can communicate quite well without them."

"Well, how am I supposed tae ask ye out?"

"You're not," she told him. "Because this insipid plan of yours is never going to work." Her voice broke on that last, and she quickly cleared her throat to cover her mistake. Damn this wolf with his sexy brogue and glowing eyes that could see right through her. He was making her long for things. Stupid things. Things she had no time for. Things she had no need for. She was the princess of her people, and they were counting on her to free them. All of this lovey-dovey crap was for those with less responsibility.

"I'll tell ye what," he said. "Give me the day tae change yer mind. Let me come help ye with whatever ye need tae do. Give me the day. And if by this evening ye dinna want tae spend time with me anymore like this, then I'll respect yer wishes."

Duana glanced away. She didn't know if she could handle an entire day of him knocking down her walls. It was too exhausting trying to hold them up.

His voice lowered until it was nearly a growl. "Kitten, I swear tae ye, I'm no' doing this out o' any misguided need tae please the prince. I'm doing this because I want ye."

His words were bold. His eyes steady on her own. Much as she tried to remain unaffected, her heart began to race. "And you don't expect to get anything out of it." Her words were too full of sarcasm to be a question.

"Oh, I do," Cedric told her as his eyes flared with heat again. "But it's no' what ye expect."

This time she didn't have to ask exactly what he meant.

She should refuse his offer. It was all completely for his own gain. He'd just admitted as much.

But was it? "Fine," she told him after a pause. "I'll agree to your proposal." Because she couldn't help herself. She wanted to see what the day would bring almost as much as he did. "But I'm telling you, I'm not going to change my mind. Not by the end of the day. Not ever."

But you will. Especially when you see what we're going to be doing this afternoon, she thought to herself.

She watched as those lips that had brought her such devastation the night before turned up into a triumphant smile. "We'll see," he told her. Then he nodded at her unfinished plate. "Finish yer lunch, kitten. And tell me what we'll be doing this afternoon."

"I need to check on my lab," she told him. "The one we set up to help me find a cure."

"I'm interested in seeing how yer tests are going."

Duana had the feeling he was only saying that to appease her. "Why? You don't believe in what I'm doing. You don't believe in me."

"Show me, then. Show me why I should."

Duana held his gaze, praying her people had found something that worked. Or even just something that would prove to him what she was doing was not a lost cause.

CHAPTER 6

A deep growl rose up in Cedric's chest as a sour scent, one he thought he'd forgotten, permeated his nose.

Duana glanced at him, her eyes flicking away again nervously, but she never faltered in her step. "I know this is hard for you," she told him. "And I want you to know that I appreciate you coming here."

Cedric glanced around the building, looking for escape routes. From the moment he'd walked in, he could smell them. The crazy ones. The soul suckers. The things he'd spent a good many years of his life hunting. And it was hard to tame his wolf, when all it wanted to do was jump through his skin and destroy them as it had been trained to do through blood and pain.

He and the princess had come to her laboratory—a large barn-like structure, quickly constructed for Duana's needs when she'd gotten permission from his pack to try her concoctions on those of her people who had been struck with the addiction. Cages made of thick iron bars lined the wall to his left. They were all full except for two. Lining the opposite were lab tables and Faeries in white coats, wearing masks, peering through microscopes. Like something you'd see in a movie. But it wasn't the crazy scientists that concerned him. It was the things in the cages. Creatures that used to be completely sane, like Duana, snarled and growled and twitched and banged their heads against the bars in an effort to get free. When they focused on him and Duana, their eyes glowed orange.

"Where did you find so many?" he asked her.

"Certainly not from you," she sneered.

Cedric smiled. His kitten was showing her claws. He much preferred this version of her.

When the fairies noticed him there all work suddenly stopped. They stared at him like he was a monster, and he had to stop and check that he hadn't suddenly grown two heads. "What are ye staring at?" he growled.

Their eyes widened and swung to Duana in perfect unison. With a wave of her hand she sent them back to work.

His nose twitched at the stench of their fear. "What are they doing?" Cedric asked her.

"They're studying blood samples," she said. We've been giving the subjects a mixture of herbs and some human drugs that have been deemed helpful for addiction, and adding a touch of faerie magic. Each subject is given different doses and then we see how they react both by observation and by drawing blood."

"And has it worked?" he asked.

A wave of sadness washed over her face. "Not yet," she told him, nodding to the two empty cages. "We've lost four already. Those ones..." She nodded to the middle group. "Are in the midst of testing a new batch. Those at the other end are new. We haven't started testing them yet."

"While I can no' lie and say I'm sad aboot it," he told her. "I ken it must be a horrible death. But it has tae be better than living like this, with a hunger that can never be appeased."

"It's not that," she told him. "It's just that I want so badly to help them." She turned to look him straight in the eye. "I've had people I cared about turn into one of these things. I've seen it firsthand. How he changed, how the hunger grows, how they can't control it. And there was nothing, nothing at all I could do to help them or to stop it."

Cedric touched her face briefly with his fingertips before his arm dropped back to his side. "Sometimes things just are as they are," he said. "And there's nothing ye can do tae change it or tae stop it."

"But that's where you're wrong," she said. "There is something I can do. And I'm doing it right now. I couldn't save the ones I cared about. But I can save someone else's loved ones. Perhaps their friends, their family. I can save them," she told him with a hard set to her jaw. "And I won't stop until I do. This is why it's so important to me that you bring those that you find to me alive. I will not do anything to risk my people or yours," she told him. "I don't even let them out of the cages. We administer everything to them through the bars and we take blood through the bars."

"That's good," he told her as a grudging feeling of respect grew within him.

She studied his expression for a moment and then turned and walked past the tables, pointing out different variations of the treatments to him, telling him what they did and didn't do, what the results had shown them. Side Effects. Different reactions. "And you were right with what you said before. The ones who died did not die quickly. It was painful to watch. There were even times, in the end, I have cut their life short myself to spare them the suffering."

"Have there been any signs o' hope at all?" he asked. His chest ached with emotions he hadn't expected to feel. Not just for Duana, but for her people. Maybe it was seeing it through her eyes. Maybe it was just the tenuous connection between them.

She turned to him and a smile lit her face. He caught his breath, unable to draw air with such a force coming straight at him. "Yes," she exclaimed. "Just yesterday. I think we had a breakthrough." She grabbed his hand without seeming to think about it and pulled him over to a table where a blonde female was looking into the eyepiece of a microscope. "Come look," Duana told him.

Cedric stepped up and stuck his eye against the lens. He saw some circles and squiggly lines and things moving around on their own, but he had no idea what he was looking at. Biology was not a subject he had ever really bothered to learn. "What is this?" he asked.

"Those are blood cells," she told him. "Humans have three main types of cells in their blood—red, white, and platelets. The Fae have an extra component in their blood. Another type of cell unique to us. I'm sure if I looked at your blood it would be quite different also. As would the vampires, etc. When the addiction is strong, this extra cell count is extremely high. Much like a surge of endorphins after you exercise. The higher it is, the more they want. What we're doing here is trying to lower that number, without the subject going through severe withdrawals."

"That's amazing," he told her. And he truly meant it.

"The trouble we're having is getting that number correct. There are two responses that can happen with an injection. One is the cell count rises too rapidly, thereby killing the subject. The other is the cell count drops too low, with the same results. Faerie blood is very tricky."

Despite his reaction when he'd first entered the barn, he found himself wondering if perhaps he'd been wrong, that maybe the princess could change things. "So, tell me, kitten, even if ye do come up with a cure, how in the world are we tae administer it tae thousands o' soul suckers before they escape? There's no way we can catch all o' them at the same time and give them a vaccine, or whatever ye want tae call it. Which means we're still back where we started. If they get out before we can seal up the portal, it will mean our lives. All o' our lives," he emphasized.

"They will go after the humans first," she said. "You know they will. That's what they do. They will go after the humans first and then they will come after your kind, then the vampires and other supernaturals, and then come after mine. It will be last. Cannibalism is not in our nature even for those as sick as these ones are." She nodded her head at the cages. "And what they do is, indeed, a form of cannibalism."

"So, are ye saying…"

"Yes, I'm saying that while they're preying on the humans, we could catch them and bring them to facilities like this where we can administer the care."

He couldn't be hearing this right. "But what aboot the humans?"

"What about them?" she asked. "Humans are disposable. They're already overwhelming the planet. We will be doing the universe a favor to let the 'soul suckers', as you call them, bring down their numbers."

Cedric stared at her, struck silent. He should be surprised by her cold-hearted nature, and yet, he wasn't. And still, it did not dim his attraction to her. She had her reasons to believe as she did. He wasn't sure what they all were, but he was sure they were there. He shook his head. "There has tae be another way." His attention drifted around the room. He watched as the scientists did their work. Then let his eyes wander over to the cages, taking in the behavior of the soul suckers locked within.

Now that Duana had told him which ones were being treated, he did notice a difference in their behaviors. The new ones were much wilder, into self-harm, spittle running down their jutting chins as they tried to escape their prison.

The ones who had been administered the last treatment, although not calm, were much less sadistic. Cedric watched as they roamed the small confines of their cell, and as he took it all in, he thought about his people, his pack, his brothers and their mates. Even the newest members, Brock and Heather and Keelin and Bronaugh, were like family to him now. Family he would not be willing to give up.

Suddenly, an idea came to him. Out loud, he said, "The prince sent Brock and Heather tae another world."

"Oh?" Duana asked without interest.

"Aye, he did. He sent them tae another world where they came across all kinds o' strange creatures. And with the flip o' a coin, the prince was able tae manipulate that world."

The princess's brandy eyes slowly made their way to his.

Cedric studied her expression. "Tis your world, is it no'? The world ye came from before ye came here. The world where the soul suckers are hidden away. The world," he said slowly. "That your kind has access tae."

"What are you trying to get at?" she said.

"I'm saying, if he can send Brock and Heather there, couldn't he send others? Ones that could administer yer cure."

She shook her head. "No, no, that's not possible."

"Why is it no' possible?"

"Because," she told him. "The addiction doesn't happen there. My people don't become this way," She indicated the cages. "Until they get to this world. In our world, they are just like me. Or any of these others here." She looked toward the researchers at the tables. "Not all Dark Fae become soul suckers," she said.

This took him aback. "Is tha' true?"

"Yes. Absolutely," she told him. "I've been here for hundreds of years. I don't have the addiction. The ones that do usually get it within the first year of being outside of our dimension."

He quickly drew the conclusion she was getting at. "So, the ones we are finding in this world now are ones tha' have escaped from yer own dimension within the last year."

"That's correct," she said.

"They're no' leftovers from the war." This explained why it was only recently they'd been spotted. And why it was only in this area of the world, where the portal had been closed.

"No," she told him.

"But how do they get out?" he mused aloud, continuing before she could answer. "The portal is weakening, aye. Or so we've been told. But it's no' weak enough that anyone could get through it. At least, that's what the lasses o' my pack have told me. Heather and Bronaugh and even Keelin." He rubbed the sides of his cheeks, feeling the beginnings of his beard. "They told me they can sense the portal weakening."

"Yes, this is true," Duana said. "I can feel it, too. And you're right. They can't get through it. Yet. But it's only a matter of time until they figure it out."

"Then how are they escaping?" he asked.

She pressed her lips together and looked away.

She was hiding something. "Duana? How are they escaping?"

"It's not me," she finally told him. "And that's all I will tell you. To tell you anymore is a risk to my own life."

Cedric studied her face and posture. He felt she was telling the truth. "Aye," he said. "Ye dinna have tae tell me anymore. I ken enough. It's the daft prince," he said.

She stared him straight in the eye and didn't confirm or deny what he had said, and he didn't expect her to.

"But why?" he wondered aloud. "Why is he doing this?"

"That's another thing I can't tell you," she told him. "I'm sorry."

The silence grew between them, each lost in their own thoughts.

She touched his arm, bringing his attention back to her. "But do you believe me now? Do you believe that I can help them?"

Taking her wee face between his palms, he told her, "I believe ye will do everything in yer power tae help yer people. I believe that ye are verra intelligent. And I believe the daft prince does no' give ye enough credit. There's good inside yer heart, Duana, whether ye want tae admit it or no'. I believe ye are strong. And I believe ye will get through this with or without me, but ken that I will do everything in my power tae help ye with this."

Her soft hands slid around both of his wrists. But she didn't pull his hands away as he would have expected. Instead color swam in her eyes. Pinks and greens and blues and yellows, even purples, shiny with moisture. "Thank you," she told him.

He watched, mesmerized, as the colors twined and separated and brightened, until a loud crash broke the spell up between them.

Duana released his wrists and stepped quickly away. "I do not want to turn and see what has happened," she called over her shoulder.

"Sorry, princess," a young male responded. "It was just an empty beaker. Nothing important."

She glanced up at him, and Cedric watched with interest as her face flooded with color before she turned away. "Thank you for all that you're doing," she told everyone. Her voice rang with the authority of her position. "I'll be back to check on you tomorrow. But let me know if anything important happens before then. You know how to reach me?"

"Yes, Princess," an older female said.

"We should go," she told Cedric. "I can see your wolf crawling beneath your skin. And it's making my people nervous."

He hadn't noticed, but aye, she was right. It wasn't the others or their work here that had the beast riled up, however. Only the wee lass who just a few moments ago was staring up at him with gratitude and hunger in her eyes. "Aye," he told her. "We should go." With one last look around, he put his hand on her lower back and escorted her from the facility.

CHAPTER 7

Duana closed the door, locking it behind her. Taking a deep breath, she leaned up against the wood and closed her eyes.

"You're home early."

"Yes, I am," she answered in a long suffering tone. "What does it matter?"

Her chin was grasped in a vise-like grip. "You know damn well it matters. It matters to our entire species; it matters to the future of our race."

Jerking her chin from his grasp, she walked into the kitchen and away from her father. "I still don't understand why it's up to me to tame your new pet. There are other ways to get him out of the picture."

The violent male from moments earlier vanished as quickly as he had appeared. Once again, a senile grin split his face. "Yes, but that way is not nearly as fun."

Duana rolled her eyes. "Are there not other games you can play? Games that don't fuck up the lives of others. Like mine?"

"Yes," the prince said. "But again, it's not nearly as fun." Crossing over to the single couch, he sat down, crossing his legs at the knees and clasping his hands on his lap. "So, tell me! How did your date go?"

Duana thought back to the picnic lunch, and the alpha's proclamation. "It was fine," she told him. "I took him to the barn. He wanted to see what I was doing."

The prince cocked his head in curiosity. "And how did he take it?"

"He asked a lot of questions, and surprisingly enough, he tried to be supportive. But he doesn't believe I can help our people. Not truly." She pressed her lips together to stop anything else from being said.

"And have you actually managed to help any of them?"

Duana looked at him in surprise. This was the first time he had shown any interest at all in what she was trying to accomplish, which really was quite surprising. Being that he was trying to accomplish the exact opposite. "No," she admitted, knowing that he would be able to sense if she lied. "I have not." Not telling him about her hope for the latest compound was not lying. It was too early for it to have any proven results.

He uncrossed his legs, slapping his knees before he stood up. "Well, I told you that was to be expected," he said. "There is no helping them once they get the addiction."

Duana sighed. "Yes, I know you did. But still, I wanted to try."

Coming over to her, he laid his hands on her shoulders and lowered his head to look into her eyes. "It will be all right, daughter. Once our people are all back in this world, where they belong. Everything will be all right."

She thought back to her conversation with Cedric. "Yes,"

she agreed. "Yes, it will." She yawned dramatically behind her hand. "I'm going to my room," she told him. "All of this stomping around in the wilderness, it makes me tired."

"All right," her father kissed her forehead. "I have some business to attend to. I'll be back late, so don't wait up for me." With a smile and a blast of air he was gone.

Duana made herself a cup of tea. While it was steeping, she opened the refrigerator, stared into it for a few seconds, and closed it again. There was never anything in there. And it wasn't like she knew how to cook anything if there was. Picking up her teacup, she wandered back to her room. She really wasn't hungry anyway despite the fact she hadn't eaten much at lunch. Her rummaging was only to distract her from her thoughts.

Colors and thoughts and emotions swirling around inside of her. And over it all, she heard Cedric's words, the ones he'd spoken at the barn.

I believe the daft prince does no' give ye enough credit. There's good inside yer heart, Duana, whether ye want tae admit it or no'. I believe ye are strong. And I believe ye will get through this with or without me...

Taking off her shoes, she padded barefoot back and forth across the creaky, wooden floor of her room. She stopped in front of her bed and stared down at the purple flowers on her comforter. But it wasn't the stitching she saw; it was Cedric's blue eyes. Everywhere she looked, they stared down at her. Making her blood rush through her veins in ways no other male ever had.

Duana couldn't recall anyone ever looking at her like that before in her life. She had never been anything but something evil. Something royal. Something untouchable, much as she longed for just the opposite.

In response, she had built a wall around her emotions. A wall that was strong enough no one could penetrate it. It kept her from getting hurt. Kept anyone from getting too close. Being of her own making, it was built well, with no cracks, no spaces of air. And yet, in two days, holes had been punched through that wall with nothing but a few kind words.

Did he mean them?

Her instincts told her he had. Could it be true? Could he really like her for who she was and not her station or what she represented? Duana's fingertips strayed to her lips, once again feeling the sweet pressure of his mouth on hers as she had a million times since the night he'd kissed her. The dark taste of Guinness and wolf on his tongue.

Her arms dropped to her sides as her room blurred before her eyes. She wanted to hate him. She needed to hate him. But she was horribly afraid he was going to make her love him.

I'm doing this because I want ye.

Low in her stomach, her womb grew heavier with each second until it was an unbearable ache. Closing her eyes, her hands wandered to her breasts, lifting and squeezing the heavy weight before they wandered down to her hips and lower...

Duana felt a rush of frustration. She didn't want this. She didn't want to bring herself pleasure. She wanted to be with someone who wanted to pleasure her. Someone who saw her the way she saw herself.

Her arms fell to her sides. But that would never be because she was "Duana, the Princess of the *an olc.*" And she had a battle to win. A battle right here within her own home to save her people.

The prince was patronizing her, thinking she would tire of playing scientist soon enough. She scoffed. That would never happen. For if she went through with what her father wanted, her people would be lost. People who depended on her, whether they knew it or not. She was the only one who could save them.

Walking over to the window she yanked the curtains closed. The sun was only just setting, but she had had enough of this day and the longings it brought with it. Longings for things she could never have. Exhausted, she stripped down to her underthings and crawled into bed.

After tossing and turning for a good hour or more, she picked up the book on her nightstand she attempted to read. But after reading the same sentence over and over and still not comprehending what the hell it was trying to tell her, she slammed it shut and set it down. Her stomach was in knots. And her mind kept going back to her picnic with the wolf.

Closing her eyes, she took a deep breath, knowing sleep would evade her this night. The dawn would bring a new day.

AFTER DROPPING Duana off at her house, Cedric needed some time to himself to think about everything he'd seen. But once he got inside his apartment, he was unable to sit still. He thought about calling Marc for some company, but then he remembered he was already out running patrols.

He missed Duncan's easygoing nature. It always managed to calm him.

Cedric sat in his chair and picked up the remote. Then he set it down again and got back up to pace in front of the window. Looking out at the evergreens towering over his apartment, he decided to go for a drive.

Not surprisingly, he found himself back in the clearing where he and Duana had had their picnic. Aimlessly, he wandered the space, not really knowing what he was looking for or even why he was there. Sitting down on his haunches, he pulled at some of the flattened grass where the they had sat and lifted it to his nose, hoping for her scent, or anything that would remind him of her.

Cedric let his arse fall into the grass and stretched his long legs out before him, leaning back on his hands. It was nice here. Peaceful, with the trees blowing in the wind and the scent of summer in his nose.

He thought about what the princess had shown him, the ones she was trying to help. He still didn't think she would be able to do it. To be honest, he didn't know what he would do if she did manage to find a cure. Allowing her kind of back into this world is not something he ever thought would happen. Duana had told him once they were here, the addiction would spread like a virus. And there was no way to control the ones who became addicted. There was no way. As much as he wanted to help, he feared he couldn't.

It came as a bit of a shock he wanted to help her now that he had heard her reasons behind it and knew more about how it happened, but he found it was true.

Cedric sat there until the sun went down, and even then, he didn't move. It wasn't until the wind picked up and the moon began to rise that he pushed himself up off the ground and went home. Grabbing a Guinness out of the fridge, he checked on his wolves, getting reports from the ones who had run patrols during the day, and making sure the ones who had the night shift were ready.

Once he confirmed all was in order, he took his beer into his room, shucked off his clothes, and climbed into bed. He didn't turn on the TV. It was already too noisy in his head despite his efforts to clear it. With one arm behind his head and his beer in the other hand, he let his thoughts drift, hoping to lull himself to sleep. Tomorrow he would be out there running drills, and he really needed to be well-rested. So for now, he pushed away all thoughts of Duana.

Gradually, the hum of the air conditioner and the sounds of the creatures in the woods behind the apartment had his eyelids growing heavy. Cedric set his beer on the nightstand, let his arm fall to his side and stared at the ceiling.

He was awoken by the brush of something soft along the side of his neck. His eyes drifted open, though he didn't remember falling asleep. It was still dark, and he had no idea how long he'd been asleep. But surely, this had to be a dream, for Duana hovered above him, the soft ends of her long dark hair brushing his chest. Her fingers chasing the trail of her lips down his jaw and over his collarbone to his shoulder.

"Am I dreaming, lass?"

She only tilted her head, her colorful eyes giving just enough light for him to see that she wore nothing but slips of white lace. The thin straps barely covered her shoulders, and the low neck-line gave him more than a glimpse of what he hungered for.

His heart began to pound as her fingers trailed over his pecs, brushing his nipples, before making their way down his ribs, pushing the blankets down as they went.

Cedric was convinced he was dreaming, so he said no

more, not wanting to break the spell. She said nothing, either. And that, more than anything, convinced him. For his kitten was rarely quiet. Och, aye. This had to be a dream.

He lay unmoving as she explored his torso, enjoying her touch. Carefully, she stood from the side of the bed where she had been sitting and placed one bonnie knee on the mattress before lifting herself up and over his prone form, straddling him low on his hips.

It was heaven itself to have her pressed against his engorged length, and without meaning to he lifted his hips, trying to get closer.

Bracing her hands on his shoulders, she leaned over and touched her lips to his. His princess tasted sweet and minty and smelled of Snowdrops. He loved her scent, and like the bell-like white flowers, she was sweet enough to eat, and yet poisonous to his soul.

The tip of her tongue touched his, tentatively at first, and then bolder. Cedric let her do as she would, reveling in the taste of her as she explored the inside of his mouth. Her hands squeezed his shoulders as her hips began to move, grinding against him.

He rolled his hips, meeting her halfway. Finding his way up the soft skin of her back to her shoulders, he pulled her hair away, wrapping his fists in the soft tendrils before releasing them to let the silky strands cascade through his fingers. Running his hands down her back, he gripped her hips, holding her still before he came and embarrassed himself. Dream or not, he would not be selfish with his pleasure.

Duana's kisses became desperate, like she feared he was about to push her away. "I just need a moment," he whispered.

She stilled beneath his palms, and when he could control himself again, he took up his exploration of her bonnie curves, cupping the round curves of her arse. Her addictive scent rose between them, made all the more sweet by the heat of her desire.

Wrapping his arms around her, he pulled her down to him until he could feel her weight on his chest. Until he could feel her heart pounding fast along with his. His breath came in short gasps as she gripped his hair, holding him where she wanted him and taking what was already hers. Even if she didn't know it.

The wisps of lace and the blankets that covered him to the waist were still between them. And it wasn't enough. He wanted to feel her skin on his. Wanted to feel each breath, each quiver, each chill or flash of heat that raced across her skin. In a flash he flipped them over, rolling her until she was beneath him. Quickly, he removed the lace from her body until she was as bare as he was.

Duana gasped as he exposed her in such a frenzy, her hands automatically covering her breasts.

He took her hands in his, and pulled them away from her body, so he could see the beauty she was trying so hard to hide. Her breasts were full, tipped with dark nipples. Her stomach was soft, no ribs poking out. Her waist sloping perfectly to hips wide enough to handle a male such as he. Shifting the blankets out of the way and unable to wait, he lowered his hips to hers. Sliding his length through her wet folds, he held his weight on his elbows so as not to crush her.

Duana moaned, lifting her hips to meet him. Still, it wasn't enough. With lips and tongue and teeth he claimed her, tasting every inch of her flesh as he made his way down to suck on her hardened nipples. A flush of heat spread across her chest, coloring her fair skin.

Images of her arse reddened from his palm flashed through his mind and he growled deep in his chest. He would like to try to tame his ferocious kitten. Not break her. Och, no. He enjoyed her spirit too much. And he would need reasons to spank her again, for he had a feeling they would both enjoy it too much to only do it once.

But for now, he just wanted to show her what was coming to mean to him, even if it was only a dream, for it was the only way she would allow. Kissing the undersides of her breasts, he roamed down her belly, spreading her legs apart with his. He couldn't wait to taste her.

As he lowered his head and found her with his mouth, Duana's fingers threaded through his long hair, holding him there. Cedric ran his tongue over every inch of her, finding the hard nub and manipulating it with his tongue. She moaned his name, encouraging him on, her thighs trembling on his shoulders.

When her cries grew louder and more desperate, he slid two fingers inside of her so he could feel it when she found her pleasure, but he was not done with her yet. Rising up onto his knees, he took himself in his hand and wet the tip in her wet heat. And when he pushed inside of her body, she was so tight, her muscles still contracting. Duana cried out as he filled her, and at the feel of her wrapped around him, his heart hammered so hard he nearly passed out.

Suddenly, she rose beneath him, took him by the shoulders and rolled them over again until she was on top. Sitting up, she took him inside of her, her head falling back until her dark hair brushed his thighs. Cedric watched as she began to move, her full breasts bouncing as she lifted her hips until the cold air of his room hit his shaft, only to be engulfed by her heat when she crashed back down. Taking him as he'd taken her.

Finding his hands, she entwined her fingers in his, stopping him from controlling their joining. Her back arched, her hips rolled seductively, her pleasure so visual Cedric was unmanned. With a yell, he crashed over the edge, his balls tightening and his cock thickening until it was right painful. He came in a heavy surge, Duana's name on his tongue as he pushed deeper inside of her. She joined him in his pleasure, coming again, her body gripping him tightly. And when it was over, she collapsed upon his chest.

His fingers tangled in her dark hair, trailing it down the soft skin of her back. He was afraid to speak. Afraid to break the spell. So, he closed his eyes and enjoyed the weight of her on his hips and chest...

Cedric opened his eyes against the rising sun, feeling as though he had been ridden hard and put away wet.

If that was the kind of dream he was going to be having he would take them. Even though he was probably going to end up with the worst case of blue balls a male had ever had. He stretched, and rolled over, having every intention of sleeping just a wee bit longer. Taking a deep breath, his entire body froze as the scent of Snowdrops filled his nose.

Cedric sat up and stared down at his rumbled bed. Grabbing the pillows he pulled them to his nose. And then the sheets. and then the Comforter. And then he leaned over and stuck his face right against the mattress.

It smelled of Duana.

Just to make sure, he jumped out of bed, left the room, opened a can of coffee, smelled it, put the lid back on, and went back into his room. He was still outside of his door when he smelled her. Cedric stilled, looking around. No one was in the apartment but him. There was just the scent of her on his blankets. And what he had dreamed had been no dream at all, but the real thing.

She had come to him.

CHAPTER 8

"How did ye find us?"

Lucian's eyes wandered lazily over the camp before they settled on the female he'd come to see. "I want tae see my son," he said.

Sara glanced around nervously as more and more shifters came out of their tents. Her expression, when she turned back to him, showed nothing. But her eyes widened slightly in warning. "He's no' here."

"Yer lying." Out of the corner of his eye, Lucian saw Thomas, the pack alpha of the Scottish Highlands, coming up on his left. He didn't say anything, just stopped about 10 feet away, his feet braced apart and his arms crossed over his chest as he observed Lucian's confrontation with Sara.

She glanced over at him nervously from the corner of her eye. "How did ye find our camp?" she asked.

"I would like tae ken the answer tae that myself," Thomas said, without looking at him.

Lucian responded, "I dinna care why yer here, or what's

going on between yer pack and mine. I only want tae see my son."

"Ye expect me tae believe that," the elder said.

"Ye need tae go, Lucian. Just go," Sara told him. "Finn isn't here."

"How can ye tell me that? Yer here, and Thomas is here. And yer mate is here, but yer son…our son…is no'?"

"That's exactly what I'm telling you." Her jaw clenched. "It was too dangerous tae bring him with us. I left him in Scotland."

"With who?"

She opened her mouth, then closed it again.

"Yer lying," he repeated. Rage rose within him and he slammed his hands into the side of his head, pacing around in a circle.

Och. He couldn't lose his temper. Not here. Not now. Lowering his arms back down to his sides, he stopped. With pleading eyes, he reached out to the female he once thought he loved. "I just want tae see my son, Sara. I've seen him for only a few brief years since the day he was born. And I did no' ken at that time that he was mine. If I had, I would have made more o' an effort. And then ye come here telling me he's mine." He paused. "Or was that only a ploy tae get me tae come with ye."

She glanced over at Thomas.

"Dinna look at him," Lucian growled. "Look at me. Me, Sara." He jabbed himself in the chest with his finger. "Can ye tell me, is the boy truly mine? Or is he no'?

After a long pause, she said in a quiet voice, "He is."

Emotion welled up in Lucian's chest, chasing away the anger. The uncertainty. Emotions such he'd never felt before.

Not even his obsessive love for Keelin could compare. "I want tae see him," he said.

"He doesn't ken ye," she responded.

"Och. How can ye say that? O' course, he remembers me! I ken he does. He called for me. That day when we were all gathered at the prince's house, he called for his Uncle Lucian. And it's time he kens the truth."

"What truth is that?" she spat. "Are ye going tae tell him his mother lied? Are ye going tae tell him how his mother lied tae ye? He will hate me."

"No, o' course no'!" he told her. "I would never poison him against ye. Yer a good maw. That's no' why I'm here."

"Why are ye here then, Lucian?" she asked. "Yer trying tae wreck our lives."

He shook his head. "No, Sara. I told ye, I just want tae see—"

"If ye see him, he's going tae ask questions I dinna have the answers tae." She scrubbed her face with her fingers. "Why now, Lucian? Why do ye have tae do this now?"

"I will no' tell him anything," he told her. "No' for forever, but for now. I just want tae see him. Make sure he's okay. That there's no' anything he needs."

"You realize," Thomas interrupted. "I could consider this an act o' war and take ye hostage right now. Or, just let my soldiers take care o' the threat now."

"I'm a threat?" Lucian scoffed. "I walked into yer camp in the middle o' the day out in the open where everyone can see me. I did no' sneak in here. I did no' make any moves o' aggression toward anyone." He turned back to Sara. "I only want tae see my son."

"Does Cedric ken yer here," Thomas asked.

Telling the truth could be the stupidest thing Lucian had ever done. But he also knew it was the only chance he had of making it out of there alive. "No," he told him. Because if he said anything else they would sniff out the lies. "No one kens I'm here. No' even my mate. I will no' tell anyone where ye are."

Thomas barked out a laugh. "Do ye expect me tae believe that?" he said. "For when it comes down tae it, ye have tae pick a side." He looked around at the others for backup. "Ye expect me tae believe yer going tae pick this pack over yer own?"

"Ye forget," Lucian told him. "This used tae be my pack. And no' all o' ye are my enemies. I have friends here. And now, my son is here. And there's no way I would ever bring any danger tae him, not on purpose. Not while I am alive. So, aye, I will keep my vow, and I will keep silent. However"—he looked over at Sara—"if he's truly no' here, then I have no reason tae do that, do I?"

He was taking a risk. They could kill him right here, right now, but they were also taking a chance that Cedric would discover where he went and what happened to him. If Lucian was dead, there was no reason for the Pacific Northwest pack to not come after them. Thomas was very brave, now that he had the prince on his side. But Lucian knew him, and he knew he was more bark than bite. And being in with the Faerie prince was a precarious position to be in. The prince did what the prince did with no explainable reasons. And Lucian had no reason to think he would forgive his death very easily. For it would mess up his latest game.

Sara watched the conversation between them, an expression of panic tightening her features when her alpha made no move to prove Lucian wrong. "My mate will no' agree with this," she said.

"I dinna give a fook about yer mate," Lucian told her. "He has nothing tae do with this. This is between ye and I."

"Yer wrong," she said, raising her chin. "He does have a say in this. He's raised that pup these last 10 years…"

"Because I did no' ken aboot him." Lucian tried to keep his voice down and failed. "I did no' ken! And it's taken me this long tae find ye when I did, or I would have been here sooner. Ye canna keep me from him forever, Sara. No' unless ye kill me. Is that what ye really want?" He stared at this female. The love was still there between them. Different now, but still there. "We have a connection between us, Sara. One that will always be there now. Are ye going tae stand there and watch them rip me apart?" he asked, throwing his arms out to the side. "Please, stand there and watch them kill the father o' your child. Will ye do that, then?"

Slowly at first, and then more emphatically, she shook her head. "No," she told him as a single tear slid over her tight features. "No, I can no'."

He took a single step toward her. "Then let me see my son."

CHAPTER 9

Duana spent the next day at the barn helping the lab technicians and watching over the experiments, hoping against hope they would have another breakthrough. She spent the day there, too. And the next. And the next.

On the fifth day. He found her there.

She was bent over one of the tables, peering through a microscope, when the hair rose straight up on the back of her neck. Still hovering over the eyepiece, she looked around. Everyone else was staring towards the door. Even some of the test subjects had stopped their incessant pacing and spitting. Duana followed the direction of their stares to find the alpha wolf, standing just inside the door, arms crossed over his wide chest, his eyes pinned to her. "I'll handle this," she told the others. "Go ahead and get back to work. We need to find out why this isn't working and we need to find out soon."

On her way to the front of the building, she stopped and checked at each table. Purposely making him wait. Biding her time so she could figure out how she was going to play this.

After she'd returned from his apartment, Duana had purposely pushed what she'd done out of her head. And the next day, when she was greeted with minor aches and pains brought on by the intensity of their lovemaking, she'd managed to almost convince herself it was from all of the hiking he was making her do. Which was, in reality, absolutely ridiculous. She was a Faerie. Nature was her home. It was enclosures such as this barn and the house's the prince insisted on living in that were unnatural to her.

But she persisted with her chosen train of thought until the memories were pushed so far down, even she had trouble believing it had really happened and hadn't just been a fleeting fantasy. There and gone for the sole purpose of appeasing her physical needs.

By the time she got to Cedric, she had a calm façade firmly in place and was able to meet his eyes like nothing had happened.

"Is this how we're playing it, then?" he asked. "Like nothing ever happened."

"I'm sure I don't know what you're talking about," she told him.

"Aye, I think ye do," he told her, dropping his arms. He reached out and ran the tips of his fingers along her jaw. "There's no need tae feel ashamed, kitten."

She flinched away. Away from the touch of those hands that had brought her such pleasure less than a week before. "I have nothing to be ashamed of," she told him.

"Then why are ye hiding from me?"

"I'm not hiding. I'm merely watching over my test subjects and helping bring about the cure we are so close to achieving."

He cocked his head to the side, his black hair in its ponytail sliding over his shoulder. "Yer hiding."

Duana's palms tingled at the memory of those dark strands gripped within her fists and she swallowed hard. He was right. She was hiding. Because she was ashamed. Not for being with him, but for being so weak that she went to him in the dead of night the way she had. She was a coward, pushing him away in the light of day. Hoping he would only remember her being there as nothing more than a dream.

"I brought ye some food. I thought ye might be hungry. You've been working a lot, and I haven't noticed ye taking any meals."

Her gaze swung sharply to his face. "Have you been spying on me?"

"Och, no. No' at all. But I'm right, am I no'? Ye've been hiding here since that night. I ken this because ye haven't been at yer house. And the fairy prince could no' tell me where you are. Like that would keep me from ye."

Her stomach was suddenly full of butterflies.

"So, come outside with me," he told her. "I will no' keep ye long, and we dinna have tae go anywhere. We can stay right here. I've got food in the car. I just want tae make sure yer fed." His eerie eyes traveled over her face. "Ye look like ye could use a break, kitten."

Duana stood, teetering on the precipice. She was starving. However, she didn't know that she was quite ready to have the heart to heart she could see he yearned for. "I can spare a few minutes," she told him. "But only a few minutes."

"Deal," he told her. With a wary look around the room, he held the door open for her and she proceeded him outside.

His black El Camino was parked a little ways away from

the barn in the shade of some trees. When they got to the vehicle, she saw he had laid out another picnic blanket for them in the bed.

"I just stopped at KFC this time. I hope that's all right with ye."

"Well, it depends on what you got," she teased.

His eyes flew to her face in surprise, and then he smiled, flashing white teeth.

As Duana's face heated, she watched him open the door. He began pulling out bucket after bucket of chicken, containers of mashed potatoes, green beans, macaroni and cheese, and a bag of biscuits. "I hope this will do," he told her. The corners of his mouth twitched.

"Is this extra crispy?"" she asked.

He reared back, obviously offended. "As if there's any other kind o' fried chicken tae eat."

Duana felt the pressures of the day lifting from her shoulders in spite of herself. This wolf certainly knew the way to her heart. Food was one of her weaknesses. If he kept this up, she truly didn't know how long she'd be able to resist his attempts to date her.

Climbing up into the bed of the truck, she settled against the side and stretched out her legs, glad she'd worn a pair of sensible, black slacks and a comfortable, coral cotton shirt. She accepted the plate he gave her, her mouth watering as soon as it was in her lap. Duana had finished off two crispy chicken legs and half of her biscuit when she noticed he wasn't eating.

She lowered her hand with the biscuit and looked up.

Cedric was sitting on the edge of the tailgate near her feet with his plate beside him, staring at her.

"What?" she asked. "Do I have something on my face?" She

swiped at her mouth with a napkin, then glanced down at the shelf of her breasts. Her shirt was clean and clear of crumbs.

"I wish ye would no' hate me so much," Cedric told her quietly.

"I don't hate you."

"Aye, ye kind o' do."

It wasn't true. She tried to hate him, but most of the time found that she could not. "Why shouldn't I?"

"Because I'm on yer side, kitten."

Duana suddenly lost her appetite. Setting her plate down on the blanket, she wiped her mouth again. "On my side? You're not on my side. You want my people dead."

"I said nothing about yer people. I said, I am on yer side."

"What does that even mean?"

"It means ye do no' need tae hate me the way that ye do, or at least the way that you try tae."

Ah. So, he could see that, too.

"I haven't forgotten who you are, Cedric Kincaid. I'd heard of you before I came here, you know. Everyone has heard of the infamous alpha of the Northwest pack who single-handedly ended the war." Duana narrowed her eyes. "No matter what you say or how nice you are to me, I know who you really are at heart."

Cedric scoffed. "Made up tales," he said. "I did no' single-handedly do anything."

"You took down more of my people than any other wolf. Your pack ended the war, small as you are. The last wolves standing."

Shadows crossed his handsome face, dimming the light within eyes. "I do no' like war," he admitted. "But I do what I have tae do—"

"To wipe out my species."

"No," he told her. "Tae save mine. And tae save the humans who were the innocent victims in all of it."

"Humans are not so innocent," she said.

"They did no' deserve tae be wiped out by mindless fairies," he argued.

"Those 'mindless fairies' are my people," she said. "My family."

Cedric stared at her; his eyes softened in sorrow. "All o' them?" he asked.

"I have no one left," she told him. And it was true. The prince was her father by birth, yes. But he wasn't hers. Not like her mother and her brother.

He dropped his eyes, then lifted them back to her face. "I'm sorry. Truly. But I can no' change what's in the past, Duana. Although I would, if it was within my power, for ye."

Heat flared across her chest and up her neck to warm her cheeks. Silence descended as Duana picked up her plate.

"Besides," Cedric said in a light tone. "I thought the chicken would soften ye up a bit. I'd heard it was yer favorite."

One didn't have to ask who had told him that little bit of information. It was true. It was her favorite. Even though she knew it went right to her hips.

Cedric gazed thoughtfully over toward the barn as he chewed. "Ye ken, the prince is no' going tae let ye do this, even if ye do find a cure."

Her food stuck in her throat and she reached for the drink he'd set beside her. When she could breathe again, she said, "Why would you tell me that?"

"Because I'm no' yer enemy, princess. No matter what ye might think of me."

"You're not my friend either," she said.

Reaching over, he took her hand in his large palm. "But I would like tae be," he said. "Verra much so." Raising her hand to his mouth, he pressed a kiss upon her knuckles before releasing her. "Again, I have tae wonder: why are ye always so suspicious o' people?"

"I'm not," she said. "Only wolves who suddenly seek out my company for reasons of their own."

"Yer company has been my fondest wish since I first saw ye sitting on that ridiculous throne next tae the prince. I would no' admit it tae anyone. No' even myself. But it is true."

Duana stared at him, unsure whether to believe what he told her, or if it was just sugary words meant to soften her up, like the chicken. She inhaled, gathering her arms around her middle in a protective gesture. "In any case, the prince won't stop me. He wants my people free as much as I do."

"Ye dinna ken this."

"Yes, I do." That much, at least, was true.

"What makes ye so sure about that?"

Glancing at her furry suitor from the corner of her eye, she decided to give him a truth, as he had done the same for her. "The prince wants to release them," she said. Catching herself, barely, before calling him her father. "He wants to release them all. The healthy ones and the sick ones. All of them." She paused. "And you're right. He does not want me to heal them. Like you, he doesn't think I can do it. It's the only reason he's allowing me to continue my work. And if I don't succeed, the sick ones will wipe out this planet, just as you fear."

Cedric paused with a spoonful of macaroni and cheese halfway to his mouth. His hand slowly lowered back down to the plate in his lap. "Aye," he said. "I do ken that."

Her head whipped around in surprise, her eyes clashing with his. "You know." Disbelief colored her tone.

"Aye," he told her. "Duncan's mate told me."

She should have known her sister would have opened her mouth. "What else did she tell you?" she asked him.

"No' much."

"Did she tell you why he wants to do this?"

Cedric resumed eating, shrugging one shoulder casually. "No, but I figured it was because he was off his head. We all ken this." Cedric nodded toward her still full plate. "Eat, kitten. I dinna want ye tae be hungry."

Actually, she was still starving. But the knots were still in her stomach from his unexpected arrival and proximity. "I find it difficult to eat amid such company," she told him.

"Well, ye better learn," Cedric told her around a mouthful of chicken. "Because this company is no' going anywhere anytime soon."

CHAPTER 10

Duncan stirred the soup cooking on the stove as Ryanne watched from her perch at the counter. "Smells wonderful," she told him.

"I could teach ye how tae make it." He glanced over his shoulder when Ryanne laughed like he'd just told a great joke.

"No thanks," she said. "I'll leave the cooking to you."

Duncan scowled at her. "Ye would think for people who are so in tune with nature that ye would ken how tae cook on a fire."

"We don't have to cook," she told him. "We just make others do it for us. Or, for the last few hundred years or so, order from a restaurant."

"What did ye do before there were restaurants?"

She cocked her head and looked off to the side. "I don't remember," she told him.

A knock at the door cut off his laughter. Duncan glanced at Ryanne, turned off the stove, and held his finger up to his lips.

She nodded, quietly getting down off the stool and walking

into the center of the living room where she would have an unobstructed view of their visitor.

Walking in that stealthy way he had that was so strange for a male his size, Duncan went to the front door and peeked out through the peephole. His shoulders instantly relaxed and he glanced back at Ryanne with a puzzled expression as he unlocked the door and swung it open.

Thinking it must be the alpha wolf who had found the house for them. Ryanne waited where she was, hoping he had some news from Cedric.

To her surprise, Keelin walked through the door.

She realized her mouth was hanging open and snapped it closed. "How did you find us?"

Keelin ran over and threw her arms around her, nearly knocking her off her feet. "I've been so worried about you," she said.

"I'm fine, I'm fine." Ryanne hugged her back, watching over Keelin's shoulder as Duncan went back to the stove. "What are you doing here?"

With one last squeeze, Keelin released her, but kept a hold of one of her hands. "I'm sorry. I know you're supposed to be in hiding and all that, but I had to come tell you." She paused a moment and caught her breath. "You need to come back. Your father is out of control."

"Well, that's not news."

"No, I mean really out of control. He's trying to mate your sister with Cedric."

"And that's a bad thing?" Duncan asked over his shoulder.

"Yes." Keelin looked at Ryanne. "Isn't it?"

"Och," Duncan spoke into the pot of soup. "Cedric has been

panting after her since he first saw her. I dinna ken what's so bad about that if it will make him happy."

"What's bad about it is that she is not keen on the idea. And if she doesn't go along with it, she's going to end up like you, Ry."

"You mean dead?"

"Yes, that's exactly what I mean," Keelin said. "He thinks the alpha wolf can control your sister."

Ryanne burst out laughing. "No one can control Duana." The idea was absurd. She had never really known her sister, as the prince had tried to kill her before taking Duana in, but she didn't need to know her to know this was true. The princess's reputation preceded her wherever she went. Ryanne sobered. "And no one can control my father."

"We can," Keelin told her.

"But not without Duana," Ryanne said. "Duana is The Lock. We need her, but she's on his side. She'd never do anything to go against him."

"That may not be true," Keelin told her.

"Soup's ready," Duncan called. "If yer hungry, Keelin, yer welcome tae have some."

"I am," she said. "Thank you."

Ryanne led her over to the counter, her mind spinning with everything Keelin had told her.

"We have some bread tae go with it," Duncan said as he set a crusty loaf on the counter. "But there was no meat. So, I apologize for that. We did have a good amount o' vegetables that I could throw together. But it's just no' the same without the meat."

He looked so crestfallen, Ryanne couldn't help but smile behind her hand.

Keelin leaned over the counter and waved a hand over his bowl. "There you go," she said.

Duncan dunked his spoon into the soup, lifting out chunks of perfectly cooked meat. "It's magic," he said in awe. Then he turned to Ryanne with an accusatory look. "Why did ye no' tell me ye could do this? I've been eating nothing but vegetables for a week!"

She laughed. "It's good for you," she told him. "It will keep you healthy and strong."

Duncan took a bite, his eyes rolling back in his head as he chewed. "A male can no' live on grass alone, lass. I need meat. Or I'll lose these muscles ye like tae fondle so much."

"Gorillas eat a total plant based diet," Keelin said. "And look at how strong they are."

Duncan's chest swelled and he pushed his shoulders back. "I am no' a monkey," he said. "I am a wolf. And wolves eat meat."

Keelin and Ryanne exchanged glances and busted out laughing.

"The soup is very good," Keelin told him a minute later in an attempt to soothe his ego. "And so is the bread."

"Yes," Ryanne agreed. "Thank the gods wolves can cook or we would be starving right now."

Duncan gave her a look that told her he could see exactly what she was doing, and she was going to pay for her insolence before he forgave her. Later. When they were alone. "How do ye two ken one another anyway?" Duncan ask.

"Keelin saved me," Ryanne told him. "I owe her my life. Literally."

"When was this?" Duncan asked.

"When my father tried to kill me," she told him.

"It was right at the end of the war," Keelin said. "I had discovered what my father was about. How he was pretending to be someone he's not. Pretending to be of the other Fae tribe so he didn't get sent into the portal. I was going to expose him for what he was. I don't know how he found out my plan, but he did, and he sent me into a trap. He sent me into a cave where he told me the rest of our family was hiding, and that he would come and get me when it was done. I couldn't pass up the chance of being with my mother and brother again, so I went into the cave. Only instead of finding my family, I found nothing but blackness and cold, wet stone. I could've kicked myself for my stupidity." Pulling herself from the memories, she looked up at Duncan. "I'd just turned around to leave again when the cave started to rumble and rock started to crumble from the walls of the cave. I ran toward the entrance, but it was too late. My father sealed off the entrance, leaving me there to die without food or water or sunshine."

"Are ye sure it was him, lass? No' just a natural cave in?"

She felt Keelin's hand on her arm. "It was my father. I saw him at the entrance to the cave right before the roof caved in and it all went black. But what he didn't know was there was another way out. It took me a while to find it, but I did. It was nothing more than a crawl space up at the top of the cave about 30 yards down this narrow crevice. Somehow, I was able to climb out..."

"And that's when I found her stumbling through the woods," Keelin said. "Months after the war had ended. I was very young. But I took her home with me and my mother and I nursed her back to health."

"So you see," Ryanne told him. "I owe her my life."

"As do I," he said.

Then he barreled around the counter, grabbed Keelin up in a bear hug, and squeezed her so tight Ryanne was afraid her ribs would crack. "Duncan, you're going to hurt her."

With a bashful look he stepped back, wiping suspicious moisture from his eyes. "This is how I was able to find Ryanne," Keelin told him.

"So, I have a question," Duncan said. "if ye were able tae find us here because yer a Fae and Ryanne is Fae, does that mean yer father can find us here? Even with the witchy words?"

"It's very unlikely," Ryanne said. "Keelin was able to find me because we share a close bond. I share no such bond with the prince. He broke it a long time ago."

Keelin smiled. "We were like sisters for many years."

"I still consider you as such," Ryanne told her. "So, what's going on with my father? Why are things escalating now?"

"I'm not sure exactly," Keelin said. "But there are vibrations happening. Bad vibrations. We all feel it."

"Is that why ye have been waking up so much at night?" Duncan asked.

Ryanne shrugged. "I've been having dreams," she admitted.

"What kind of dreams?" Keelin asked.

"Nothing I can put my finger on," she told her.

"I think the time is coming," Keelin said. "I think it's coming faster than we were prepared for. Your father is going to release them into this world. All of them."

Ryanne stood up. "No, he won't." With a look at Duncan, she headed toward their bedroom. She was going to miss this house, with all of the love and peace. But she couldn't let this happen.

They couldn't let this happen.

"Where are ye off tae, lass?"

"To pack," she called. "It's time we went back."

"But it's no' safe." Duncan was right behind her.

"It's the safest it's gonna get," she told him. "And my father needs to be stopped."

"How are we going to get Duana over to our side?" Keelin asked as she pulled open a drawer and started throwing clothes on the bed.

"I don't know," she told her friend. "But we will."

CHAPTER 11

A month had gone by since Cedric set out to court the princess. He took her out whenever he wasn't on patrol. Sometimes it was to a public place, but mostly not. The majority of the time he took her somewhere where they could be alone. Where he could try to break down her defenses and get her to trust him. If there was too much hubbub going on his wee kitten tended to use that as a way to avoid talking to him. So far, whenever he seemed to be making any strides with her it was, as the old saying goes, one step forward and two steps back.

He tried to woo her with tales of his childhood, for she would ask him questions about growing up. She would ask these questions quite a lot and it led him to believe there was a reason she asked these questions so much. And he'd come to the conclusion it was because she had not grown up with a family as he had. She grew up with first her brother as the war brewed between the tribes, and then the crazy Prince. So, he answered her questions and told her tales that made her laugh.

But whenever he would ask her questions about her life growing up, she would duck and cover and turn the conversation back to him.

Of course, this was when she wasn't spewing insults or cutting him down or refusing to go spend time with him at all.

He'd asked her once about the night she came to his room. And she'd stared at him like he'd just grown another head. "You have very vivid dreams," she told him.

"It was no dream, princess. Ye were there. I ken this because I smelled ye there the next day. Just like I can smell ye now."

"So, you're saying I stink," she said.

Cedric had pushed down his frustration at the way she fought him at every turn. "I'm no' saying ye stink," he'd said. "Ye smell better than anything I've ever smelled in my life. A mixture o' woman and Snowdrop flowers.

She'd arched one brow. "Snowdrop flowers," she'd repeated.

"Aye, from my homeland."

And then she had asked him about what it was like the first time he'd transitioned and succeeded in changing the subject once again.

Cedric pressed her on it another time, trying to get her to admit that she had come to him, to admit to the feelings they had shared, admit to the intimacy. But instead of acknowledging what had happened, she'd gotten angry and faded into their surroundings before running away, leaving him sitting alone on a park bench watching the water babble over the rocks.

After that, Cedric stopped trying to get her to admit to what happened. And just tried to get her to not be so angry all the time. Because he knew her anger for what it was: it was a defense mechanism. A wall she'd erected to keep him from getting close to her.

The question was…why?

That is not to say there weren't things he had done. Things that, until that first dinner at the restaurant, he'd had no idea what it would cost for her and for him. Things that shamed him then and now, but things he could not go back and change. Although he would if he could, because if she ever found out, she would hate him for it. Truly hate him. And she would never forgive him.

This was something that Cedric could not live with. Because although she showed her claws to him often and fiercely, he knew she did not hate him as much as she claimed. For if she did, she wouldn't still be seeing him. Much as she grumbled about it, she still came every time he appeared at her home or her lab. She still talked to him. Spent hours with him. And the more he got to know her, the more he found he did not hate her, either. Och, no. Not at all. Her feisty attitude and sharp words excited his wolf, and Cedric often found himself readjusting things in his pants.

But that's all there was. There was no more touching. No more kissing. She held him at arm's length and kept him there with the flash of color in her eyes and the tightness of her jaw, despite the fact she burned for him, too. The princess could deny it all she wanted to, but there was no mistaking the scent of her desire or the sound of her speeding pulse.

He had the feeling it wasn't him she was afraid of, but more herself, because the attraction was there. An intriguing scent that rose between them when they were sparring back and forth with words and accusations. A scent that mixed with her sweet smell and made him growl deep in his chest with need, making her eyes flash up to his, a kaleidoscope of colors that never failed to mesmerize him.

And yet, still, she pushed him away.

A knock at his apartment door interrupted his thoughts. "Come in!" Cedric called.

The door opened, and Marc's scent hit him before the broad shoulders and long legs of his most serious wolf came around the corner.

Cedric raised his chin in greeting and Marc did the same.

"Are ye going out again?" Marc asked, eyeing up Cedric's black jeans and his red, button down cotton shirt.

"I am," Cedric told him as he finished pulling his hair back, fastening the ponytail with a black band.

"Are ye having any luck with yer princess?" Marc asked.

"Hard tae say. The princess is a tough shell tae crack."

Marc raised an eyebrow. "It must be true, for it's been, what? A month now? Within the first week my Bronaugh was taking off her clothes and seducing me in the woods."

Cedric rolled his eyes. "Ye dinna have tae rub it in," he told him.

"Maybe she just does no' like you."

"Ye've tried that one before," Cedric responded. "And I'll tell ye again, that's no' the way. She does like me. Or at least her body does." He grinned knowingly.

Marc held up his hand. "I dinna need tae ken anymore."

"I wasn't going tae tell ye anymore." But then the smile fell from Cedric's face. He released his breath on a long exhale. "Because there is no' any more tae tell. My wee kitten has sharp claws, and she uses them tae keep me at my distance. The few times I've managed tae get too close, whether physically or mentally, she takes a swipe at me." He made a gesture with his hands like a cat clawing at its prey. "But at least she does no' 'poof' away."

"'Poof'?" Marc asked.

"Aye, 'poof'," Cedric said, not in the mood to have his choice of dialect criticized. "'Tis the only way tae explain it and ye well ken what I mean. Just like the prince 'poofs' into my apartment whenever he wants."

Helping himself to a beer out of the fridge, Marc sat down on the nearest barstool and turned it to face Cedric in the living room.

Cedric noticed him wince as he lowered his weight. "What's the matter with ye? Did ye get hurt last night?"

"No' the way ye think," Marc said. "It was my Bronaugh. Aye." He answered Cedric's questioning look. "We got a little carried away," he said. "And I tweaked my back. But it'll be fine in a few hours." Taking a long swig of his beer, Marc balanced it in his lap between his hands. "So, what are ye going tae do? If the princess won't heel, the prince will no' be happy."

"There's no' much I can do," Cedric said. "She'll either want tae be with me, or she will no'. I canna change her mind either way. The only reason I've stuck around this long is because I ken...no...I *feel* deep down inside that she's no' so against my company, but is putting on a show. I just can no' figure out the reason why."

Marc wiped his mouth with the back of his arm. "Well, ye better bring her around before long. Things are getting more and more dangerous out there as more and more soul suckers are finding the cracks in the portal. So far, we've managed tae keep them contained tae this area. But that's no' going tae last for long. There's only so many of us. Even with all o' us and a few neighboring packs, there's only aboot one hundred o' us wolves. We barely have time tae eat or rest. See our females."

Cedric sunk down into his favorite chair with his boots still in his hand, but he didn't try to put them on. Marc was right. He was running out of time.

What would the prince do if he couldn't get Duana on his side? He knew the crazy fool was counting on him to keep her under control and to keep an eye on what she was doing. But whenever he asked her for updates on her research or suggested going back to the barn himself to see how things were going, she shut him down fast and would only give him vague answers to his inquiries that didn't tell him anything other than they are working through it.

"Also," Marc told him. "Bronaugh and the other females are telling me the prince is getting more and more chaotic. Or at least he seems tae be. That there's a method tae his madness. They dinna ken what it is, though."

"What do ye mean?" Cedric asked.

"They said he's disappearing for long periods o' time. And once when Heather and Brock went tae his house because he had invited Heather over tae visit with her, Brock caught her before she could knock because he heard voices inside. Listening at the door, they overheard the prince talking tae some o' his henchmen. He could no' hear everything," Marc said. "But he picked up enough tae ken that the prince is losing patience. And he's trying tae think o' ways tae accelerate the opening o' the portal."

"He canna do that," Cedric said. "Duana is no' ready. She will no' be able tae save her people."

"I dinna think he wants the people saved," Marc told him. "I think he wants the soul suckers out. I think he wants them to take over the world."

"I learned something from the princess," Cedric said. "Something I did no' ken before about her kind."

"Wha's that?"

"Her people do no' develop the addiction until they come here, tae our world. And," he continued. "No' all o' them will get it. The ones who do become soul suckers within a short time after coming here."

Marc got up from his stool and walked over to him.

Cedric looked up to find his dark eyes intense on his face.

"So, my Bronaugh…"

Cedric rose to his feet. It hadn't even occurred to him! "Och, aye. I dinna even think o' it! Aye!"

"She's no' in danger o' turning into one o' them?"

"No. No, no' from what Duana told me."

Marc swayed on his feet, and Cedric caught him by the elbows and gently lowered him onto the couch, setting his beer on the table. "I dinna ken what's going on with yer lass, but she will no' turn."

"Thank the gods. Thank the gods, Cedric." Marc gripped his forearms as his eyes swam with tears. "I've been preparing myself, ye ken. Secretly, I've been preparing myself tae lose her. And I dinna ken how I was going tae be able tae do it."

"Ye will no' have tae, my friend. Whatever is going on with Bronaugh, this is no' it."

Cedric sat back down and waited for him to compose himself. He felt Marc's emotions almost as if they were his own.

"So, the prince wants his people out en masse, because he hopes that they a good majority o' them will turn." His expression became stricken. "He kens what he's doing. They will overrun th' world, Cedric. This is what he wants. And he's been using us tae get it." He suddenly frowned. "But then, why is he allowing the princess tae find a cure?"

A horrible feeling came over Cedric, raising the hackles on the back of his neck. Because he knew Marc was right. The prince wouldn't let anyone stop him. Not even his own daughter. "He's going tae kill her," Cedric said. He was surprised at the eerie calm that overcame him. "That's why he's trying tae mate her off tae me, so he'll have an excuse tae tell his people. He wants tae kill her just like he plans on killing all o' us."

"And he can say she betrayed them."

He raised his head and met Marc's eyes. "I need tae warn her," Cedric told him.

"I ken that would be a good idea," Marc said.

CHAPTER 12

Less than an hour later, Cedric was knocking on the door to the prince's house. Unlike the first few times he'd taken her out, the door swung open almost immediately, and his princess stood before him.

Cedric swallowed hard, his mind going blank, momentarily forgetting the danger she was in as his eyes roved over her curvy form. He had told her they were going out someplace nice and she had dressed the part, wearing a red slip of a dress that clung to her hips and breasts, creating interesting shadows and valleys every time she moved.

Her hair was long and loose, falling in soft waves over her shoulders. And her large, brandy-colored eyes brightened to soft pinks and greens and blues as they took in his own attire.

The night was cool, even though summer was fast approaching, and he stood there like a fool watching how the dress clearly outlined her thick, bonnie arse and thighs when she turned to get a soft, creamy wrap, her heels clicking on the floor in sync with his pulse.

He couldn't get his feet to move for a good long time after watching her curvy ass walk away. And the view coming back was even better. She may have said something to him. She may not have. He couldn't have said one way or the other, although he thought he saw her lips form words.

Taking a deep breath, he cleared his throat and tried to focus on what she was saying.

"Are you just going to stand here all night blocking the door or are you going to feed me?"

He had something to feed her all right. And food had nothing to do with it.

One eyebrow arched as though she'd read his thoughts. Cedric cleared his throat again. "Aye, lass, we're going tae dinner. But first, I need tae talk tae you."

"About what?"

Cedric looked over her shoulder, his eyes roaming the empty rooms behind her. "Is the prince at home?"

"No," she said. "He's been gone for hours and I don't know when he's coming back. Why? Did you need to see him?"

"No." Cedric shook his head. "Just you. But I canna tell ye here." Even though he was gone, he could poof in any moment. Or he could be listening. Reaching out, he took her hand as he often did now. It was the only contact she would allow.

"Can't we just talk about it over dinner?" she asked as he all but dragged her out of the house.

"I'd rather no' tell ye what I have tae tell ye with so many people around."

The princess dug in her heels—quite a feat with the height and pointy-ness of them—and refused to go any further. "I think you need to tell me whatever it is you need to tell me right here and right now," she demanded.

"I can no' do it, princess. I can no' take the chance the prince will come back. Please, just come with me. And then after I tell ye, if ye still want tae go have dinner with me, I will buy ye all the fancy meals ye would like. And if ye don't, I'll buy them for ye, anyway. But I'll get them tae go so ye can take it home and eat yer fill."

"And what about you?" she asked.

"I will do whatever ye wish me tae do." And he realized in that moment the truth of those words. He would do anything she needed him to do. Anything she wanted him to do. All she had to do was crook her finger, and he would come running.

And that was when he realized that for all his plans to seduce the princess, it was she who had seduced him. Physically and emotionally.

Duana stood for a moment, not moving, searching his face. She must have seen something there to convinced her she needed to hear what he had to say. For finally, she said, "All right, let's go."

With sadness in his heart, he nodded at her fashionable shoes. "Ye may want tae bring some sturdier shoes for this part."

When she returned wearing flat-soled shoes, her heels dangling from her fingers, Cedric helped her into the car. Neither one said a word as he drove them to the clearing where they'd had their first picnic. The sun was just setting when they got there, it's light dappled through the trees and leaving pretty patterns on the ground. But to the east he could see the clouds rolling in, bringing a summer rainfall that reflected his mood. The ominous clouds a forbearing of things to come.

Once again, there was no one else there traversing the trail, which was why Cedric liked to come here. The humans who had found this place tended to come in the early morning hours, getting their exercise before they went off to their day jobs and such.

Duana stopped walking and pulled her hand away before they reached the clearing, crossing her arms over her chest. Cedric fought to keep his eyes off of the sweet swells of womanly curves that pushed up above the V neckline of her dress. "What is it that you needed to tell me so badly?" she asked. "And don't beat around the bush. I'm starving."

He looked around; they were far enough down the trail that no one would see them. Per her wishes, he got straight to the point. "I think ye are in danger, kitten."

"Danger from whom, exactly?" she asked.

"From the prince," he said.

"That is not news to me," she told him calmly. "The prince is not in his right mind. It's been this way since I first met him and has only been getting worse over the years. I'm always in danger. I'm just waiting for him to snap one day and send me off back to our world."

"I think that day has come," Cedric said. "Because I ken now why the prince is trying tae push ye off on me."

"Because he wants to keep an eye on me," she said. "We discussed this on our first date."

It caught his attention how she didn't cringe anymore at words like "date." "It's more than that," he told her.

"Just spit it out," she ordered.

"Duana, the prince is planning tae release yer people from the dimension they are locked in."

She looked at him like he was the one losing his mind. "Yes, I know this. That is why I'm working on the cure."

"He does no' want ye tae come up with a cure," he told her. "He wants them tae do what they will do naturally—take out the humans, and then take out us, and every other creature until it is only the Dark Fae."

She shook her head. "It won't get that far. I will have a cure by then. And I will be able to save not only my family but many of the others, if not all."

"I do no' think ye will," he said. "The prince isn't going tae give ye time tae get a cure. The prince does no' want them tae be saved. He does no' want ye tae be saved. That's why he's trying tae pawn ye off on me. Because he plans tae kill me and my pack. And he plans tae kill all o' our mates." He paused, willing her to understand. "He plans tae kill all o' the Fae who do no' fall in line with the new world. With his new world."

"I don't believe you," she told him. "I've been with the prince for a long time. If he wanted me dead, he could have done so a long time ago. Like he did with my sister."

"Yer right." Cedric pondered what she'd just said. "And I honestly dinna ken why he hasn't yet. I dinna ken why he keeps you around."

"Because he's lonely," she told him.

"Aye, that may be. But I ken he will rid himself o' ye, eventually, because he wants tae rule the world. and he can no' rule the world if he has anyone competing for his throne." He walked away, his mind spinning. How to convince her? "He had your brother killed." Cedric regretted the words as soon as they left his mouth. His kitten would never forgive him. But her life was far more important to him than her forgiveness.

"That's not true. My brother was killed during the war. Fighting things like you." Her mouth twisted in disgust.

"Yer brother died fighting one thing like me. Yer brother

died fighting me," he told her. A weight lifted from his chest as the truth came out.

Duana stared at him, her eyes blank and free of colors as she struggled to comprehend what he was saying to her.

"It was right after the war had ended," Cedric told her. "After everything was done and there should have been peace. The prince told me there was a faerie who was trying tae release all o' the *an olc* we had just gotten through the portal. He told me that all those years o' fighting would be for nothing if this one male succeeded in what he was trying tae do. And I believed him." Cedric paused, the words sticking in his throat. "He sent me tae take him out. And that is what I did," he told her. "Tae reinforce the alliance with yer prince and his kind. When I got tae the location where the portal was closing, I found a male Fae in a battle with wolves from the Idaho pack. This one male was verra powerful, and the wolves were hurt. I could see they weren't going tae last much longer. So, I jumped in on the fight. And I...I killed him." Cedric didn't say any more about it. She didn't need to know the gory details of how her brother had died. "I can tell ye it was a quick death," he told her. "He did no' suffer. I swear it. I do no' believe in making anyone suffer, no matter what they may have done."

Duana still stared at him with no expression on her face, her eyes cold and hard. When long moments passed and she still didn't say anything, Cedric took a step toward her.

Pain stabbed through him, like sharp pieces of shrapnel. Her pain. He'd known that the tender beginnings of their relationship would not survive through this confession. He knew this. And yet, deep down, he had hoped that they had made enough of a connection that she would know he wouldn't have done what he had if he had known her. That he wouldn't have done what he had if he had known, way back then, how it would affect their future. That, somehow, she would understand all of this, and she would forgive him for what he had done. Would know how much it had cost him to confess this to her, the female he loved, in order to save her life.

Duana took a step back, then another, purposefully putting space between them. Even that minor separation felt like hands tearing his heart out of his chest and he stepped forward and fell to his knees before her. "Please do no' hate me," he begged. "I ken that's tae much tae ask, but I'm asking. Please, Duana, do no' hate me. I did no' ken who this male was. And I did no' ken ye or what he was tae ye. But what I do ken…what I realize now…is that he was no' trying tae open the portal. He was trying tae escape into it. He had hurt my kin only tae make them let go o' him so he could get away. He was running for his life. And I took that life," he said quietly. "As I've taken many others. And I've never felt guilty aboot it. I've never felt one iota o' remorse."

"What do you feel now?" she asked him calmly. Too calmly.

"I feel that I deserve yer hatred. I deserve this pain. I deserve tae live a life without ye in it." He looked up at her, blinking his eyes to try to see through the sudden moisture in them. "Ye are meant for me, kitten," he said. "Ye and me, we are meant tae be together. We've been playing this game o' cat and mouse, and it's been fun. But I'm done playing games. I ken this, from the first moment I saw ye. And it has nothing tae do with what you are or what I am or what the prince wants, and everything tae do with the fact that ye are my life mate and I am falling deeply in love with ye. So please kitten, put yer claws away, just this once and talk tae me."

She looked at him like he was a bug she wanted to squash

beneath her. "Talk to you?" she asked. "I can't even stand to look at you right now."

"Duana." Cedric reached for her, but his hand grabbed nothing but thin air.

He scented the air. Her now familiar cool scent lingered on the air for a brief moment before being swept away on the humid breeze. His princess was gone. And he knew she wasn't coming back.

CHAPTER 13

Duana stood motionless in the center of the living room of the house she shared with the prince. Her father.

Her lips twisted as a sour taste filled her mouth.

Prince.

He wasn't a prince. He was a murderer.

The numbness she'd felt since she'd left Cedric was burned away by a sudden swell of fiery rage. It filled every cell of her body, a jolt of light keeping her alive. She didn't even feel sad, although she was sure that would come later. All she felt was a destructive rage boiling inside of her until she felt like it was about to burst from her eyes and nose and ears in her body's effort to release it.

With no one else to unleash it on, she turned that rage toward the house surrounding her. The single couch flew through the air, slamming into the wall with such force it shattered into multiple pieces. Throwing her fist into the air, she sent a wave of energy so fast and so hard it tore through the sheet rock and brick and hit a car passing on the street outside, sending it flying into the house across the street.

She didn't stop to see if the driver and the occupants of the house were okay. She didn't care. They were only humans.

The floor trembled beneath her feet as she marched into the kitchen, tearing cabinets from the wall and pulverizing the kitchen table and chairs with little more than a thought. Blue electricity teased the tips of her fingertips, and with the swing of her hand she sent it in an arc around the room, tearing more holes through the walls and old and unused appliances.

When there was nothing left to destroy, she gripped the hair on either side of her head and pulled, screaming, as she fell to her knees. Her rage spent, the loss of her brother overwhelmed her, as fresh as it was the day she'd lost him.

The day Cedric had killed him.

Please, Duana, do no' hate me. I did no' ken who this male was. And I did no' ken ye or what he was tae ye. But what I do ken...what I realize now...is that he was no' trying tae open the portal. He was trying tae escape into it. He had hurt my kin only tae make them let go o' him so he could get away. He was running for his life...

She slammed her hands over her ears, as if that could block out his pleas for forgiveness.

Her father had ordered his only son murdered. Her only brother. The sibling she'd grown up with. He had cared for her. Loved her.

Had given her over to the only male he knew who could protect her, even knowing that same male would soon have him fighting for his life.

And once he was gone, she was nothing but a pawn in the prince's game. They all were. Chess pieces he moved around at will. Even Cedric.

Especially Cedric.

A sob tore through her. What it must have cost him to make that confession to her. She knew how much he cared about her. She saw it every time he looked at her, his eyes burning with white fire. She felt it every time he gently guided her into a restaurant with his hand on her lower back. She heard it every time he growled her name.

Her fucking father had known exactly what he was doing when he'd brought them together. This was why he'd insisted she be there beside him. Why he'd encouraged her to work on her cure, knowing she would need to enlist the help of the wolves to capture her subjects.

And when he'd seen the attraction between them, he'd set his plan in motion. And for what? To torture them both further.

Well, she was done being his pawn.

Now she just had to figure out what move to make next, before he made it for her. A blanket of calm fell over the princess as she kneeled on the floor. Slow and steady, she got to her feet and turned until she faced the front door. A moment later, the prince appeared out of thin air just inside the door. He was smiling.

He walked in, past the broken furniture, past the holes in the wall. Without giving them a second glance, he greeted her. "Hello, daughter. I wasn't expecting you home so soon! I do hope you didn't have another quarrel with your beau." It wasn't until he tried to set his hat on the non-existent counter that he stopped what he was doing and looked around the room. "Whatever happened here?" he asked. "Or maybe I shouldn't ask," he told her with a devilish twinkle in his eyes. "Where is your wolf suitor, by the way? Hiding in a closet, perhaps?" He frowned, raising his fingers to his lips. "No, no. He wouldn't fit in any of the closets in this house. He's too large…"

"Why did you kill my brother?" Duana asked him.

The prince became perfectly still at the question. "I'm sorry?" he asked.

"Why-did-you-kill-my-brother?" She enunciated each word loud and clear.

"Oh, but I didn't kill your brother," he argued. "Your brother was killed by wolves."

"Wolves that you sent."

He narrowed his eyes, all silly demeanor gone as though it had never been. "Who told you this?" he asked her.

"It doesn't matter," she told him. "Now tell me why you killed my brother. He was no threat to you. He was trying to escape. He didn't want to stay in this world."

With a wave of his hand, the prince righted one of the fallen chairs that was still somewhat intact and took a seat. Resting his hands on the head of his cane that stood between his legs, he tilted his head, his long, white hair slithering over one shoulder. "Your brother was the next in line for the crown," he told her.

"For the Dark Fae crown," she interrupted.

"For the only crown," he corrected. "I've decided the two different tribes of Fae will be no more. It's silly, really. We're all magical creatures of the forest. Light magic…dark magic…why differentiate? Magic is magic. We need to learn to get along. So there will be only one leader. And that is me."

"And the best way to achieve this, is to remove any competition." Duana concluded. A sudden thought occurred to her. "Is that why you killed Ryanne?" she asked him.

"Ryanne was out of control," he told her. "She had crazy

ideas. She had to be removed for the good of all of our people." He gestured toward Duana. "You saw it yourself. She wanted to murder her own father!" He had the gall to look disturbed by the notion.

"And my brother?" she reminded him. "What threat was he? He was trying to escape. To go back to our world. He didn't want your precious crown."

"Your brother would have come back eventually, and he would have challenged me for the crown. And that I cannot allow."

She stared at him, this man who had been a teacher to her. This man who, for the first 20 some years of her life, she knew only as the prince of the *na maithe* tribe. It wasn't until years later that she found out he was her father and not *na maithe* at all, but *an olc*, a Dark Fae. "So, what about me?" she asked him. "I am the official princess of the *an olc* tribe. That makes me a bigger threat to you than anyone. So, what about me, father?"

His eyes flashed to hers. It was the first time she had called him "father."

"Are you going to kill me, too?" She held up a finger. Halting his words before he could say them. "Wait, don't answer that, yet," she said. "What I'm really curious about is why you haven't killed me already. Why keep me around?"

"Because family is important," he told her. "And you were the only one I had left."

"Because you killed my brother and sister." She tried and failed to keep the astonishment from her voice.

"And I regretted it the moment it happened. Both times," he told her, banging his cane on the floor in emphasis. "Besides, you are the only one who is truly my child," he told her. "You think like me. You act like me. Saving our people is the most important thing to you, just like it is to me. Even if we do have different ideas on how to go about it."

"Then why are you trying to pawn me off on the wolf?"

"Because, my dear, it's the only way to control these crazy ideas you've been having lately."

"What crazy ideas?" she asked.

"This idea of yours that you can somehow cure my creations." He smiled. "Don't think I don't know about it."

"I'm sorry?" she asked. Surely, she hadn't heard him correctly. "And of course you know about it. I told you."

He smiled, his expression patronizing. "You didn't think this addiction came about accidentally, did you?" Then he laughed, loud and bold. "Oh no, my sweet daughter. I created the"—holding up his hands, he made air quotes—"soul suckers."

Duana's blood ran cold, his words chilling her to the bone. "Why the hell would you create something like that? We lost half of our tribe. I lost my mother!"

"Yes, and that was a sad repercussion that could not be avoided."

"Did you do that to them?" she asked.

"No no no." He shook his head. "No, they just happen to be one of the weak links."

A weak link. Her mother was a weak link.

Duana was not going to be a weak link.

"Well, your little plan to mate me off to the wolf is done," she informed him. "I will not be seeing him anymore."

The prince appeared utterly flabbergasted by that news. "But I thought you were getting along so well!"

"We were," she told him. "Until he confessed to me that he was the one who killed my brother. Under your orders."

"Well, surely you can't blame him for that," he said. "After all, he was acting under my direction."

"I can and I will," she insisted. "I'm done with the alpha wolf. I'm done with you," she said. Duana averted her eyes as she passed him on the way to her room. He did not exist for her anymore.

"But where are you going?" the prince called after her.

"To pack," she said. "I'm leaving."

She was down the hall and about to enter her room when the prince appeared in front of her. "I'm sorry, my dear. But I'm afraid I cannot allow that."

"You cannot stop me," she told him.

He gave her a pitiful look. "This would have worked out so much better if you had just mated the alpha wolf like I had instructed." He sighed. "Now, there are going to be questions, and I'm going to have to answer to the rest of the tribe when they ask me what happened to their Princess. It will be harder for them to accept me as their true leader now. But I am *an olc* after all, so I guess they really don't have a choice, as I will be the only royal member left to rule."

Duana's heart pounded within her chest. It was at that moment she truly realized Cedric had been right, her own father would kill her over some misguided notion that she was a threat to his crown.

His eyes hardened, turning completely black.

Without making any sudden moves or gestures to alert him, Duana laid her palm on his weathered cheek. "I'm so sorry I'm causing you all the trouble, father."

"The youngest always do." His sad smile froze on his face as Duana sent everything she had into the side of his skull.

Blue lightening lit up his skin cells, making them transparent as her magic made its way into his neurons. She thought she saw a flicker of pride in his eyes right before they closed.

Prince Nada fell heavily to the wooden floor.

Duana stared down at him. He wasn't dead. A little jolt would never kill one as powerful as her father. But it would keep him down long enough for her to get out of there and catch a taxi.

Bending down, she rummaged through his pockets, sending up a silent thanks when she found two crumpled twenty dollar bills in his inside jacket pocket.

The next thing she knew, she was standing in the middle of Cedric's living room, staring at her dead sister in horror.

CHAPTER 14

After the princess had left, Cedric remained on the path, on his knees, until the rocks dug through his jeans and into his skin. And even then, he didn't rise. Not right away. He couldn't.

Gradually, he realized his phone was vibrating in his pocket. Pulling it out without really thinking about it, he glanced at the screen. Marc had texted him, urging him to hurry home.

His mind blank and his body numb, he pushed himself to his feet and strode back to his car. As he hurried back to the apartments, he didn't think of his confession to Duana. Refused to be cognizant of what his life would now be like without her. He just drove, his mind carefully blank.

Later, when he was alone, he would let the fallout hit him. But not now.

When he walked through his front door, he was shocked to see Duncan and Ryanne along with the rest of his pack and their mates. Even Bronaugh was there. His hackles went up

133

when he saw her. Her blonde hair was mussed and she had dark circles under her glowing red eyes.

Dragging his attention from her, he turned to Duncan. "What are ye doing here? Yer supposed tae be in hiding." He shook his head before his friend had a chance to answer. "It's no' time yet." Then he threw his arms around him and hugged him close. "It's good tae see ye, Duncan."

Duncan hugged him hard, adding a few thumps to his back for good measure. "But it is," he said. "Keelin came tae see us…"

Cedric found her small form half hidden behind Lucian. "Ye went tae see them? he asked. "How? How did ye ken where they were?"

"Faeries can always find one another," Heather told him. "Especially if they have a close bond."

"Ye have a bond." He looked back and forth between Keelin and Ryanne.

"We do," Keelin answered.

"Keelin and her mother saved me when my father tried to kill me."

"Long story," Keelin said. "For another time. But right now, what you need to know is that time is running out. The prince is getting tired of waiting. He's going to make his move. And he's going to do it very soon."

Suddenly, all eyes looked over Cedric's right shoulder.

She's here. Duana was in his apartment. He knew it without looking. He felt her in his blood and in his bones. Gathering his emotions and shoving them down deep, he turned around.

The princess stood not four feet behind him. She was staring at Ryanne like she had seen a ghost.

"Duana. What is it? What's wrong?"

"He's going to kill me," she told him without taking her eyes from her sister.

"Welcome to the club," Ryanne said.

Bronaugh spoke up, her voice dark and husky. "We need to get her out of here," she told Cedric. "He will follow her. He can track her."

"It's true," Duana told him, finally tearing her eyes away to clash with his. "He will find me and he will kill me. Or he'll make somebody else do it. He admitted it to me, not thirty minutes ago. But I got away..." Her voice trailed off. "I didn't know where else to go."

Cedric closed the distance between them. "Och. O' course ye should have come here." Hatred for her father welled within his chest, pure and cold and unlike anything he'd ever felt before. "I will no' allow anything tae happen tae ye, kitten."

"The cabin," Lucian said. "We can take her tae the cabin. It's still warded. Is it no'?"

"Aye. Aye, it is."

Keelin stepped forward. "I'll take her there."

"No," Ryanne said. "I will." She put her hand out to Duncan and he tossed his keys to her. Then she took Duana's hand.

Cedric reached out to touch her hair, but she was gone.

"Duncan," Marc said. "We need tae hide Duncan."

But he was already halfway to the front door. "I'll hide out in the woods until he's gone." He looked at Marc. "Come and get me when ye can."

Marc gave him a nod and Duncan was gone.

Not twenty seconds later, the prince appeared.

Within that time, Cedric, Marc, Lucian and Brock had all grabbed beers out of the fridge and they were sitting in the living room with a taped football game on while Heather, Keelin and Bronaugh chatted at the kitchen counter.

When Prince Nada appeared directly in front of them, Cedric frowned, waving him out of the way. "Yer blocking the game," he told him.

The prince turned around and gave the TV a cursory look, his white eyebrows drawn down in confusion. "It's not football season," he said.

"Brock recorded it for me," Cedric told him. "This was my team's best game last season and I missed it. Thanks tae ye."

The prince didn't step out of the way. "Where is she," he asked.

"Where's who?" Cedric asked him.

He glanced over at Heather and Bronaugh, their heads bent together over an open magazine, then at Keelin, standing in front of the open fridge door. She started pulling food out. "You know very well who I'm speaking of, wolf. Where is the princess?"

Cedric shrugged. "I canna tell ye." He sighed heavily and allowed a trace of sadness to bleed through in his voice. "It's no' working out between us. So yer just going tae have tae think o' a different way tae keep an eye on her."

The prince stayed where he was. Cedric felt him probing around in his head and he let him do it, keeping his thoughts on football, until finally, Cedric threw his hands up. "Either grab a beer or get out o' the way!"

In a flash, the prince was gone.

The wolves stayed where they were for a few more minutes, exchanging side glances. But none of them did anything other than cheer on their team. Heather, Keelin and

Bronaugh took nervous sips from their own drinks as they waited.

Cedric looked over at the females. When Keelin gave him a nod, he turned off the TV and all four males stood up.

"I have tae go tae her and make sure she's okay," he told them.

"O' course," Marc responded. "We'll stay here. I'll text ye if anything happens."

Grabbing his keys from the counter, Cedric took off out of the apartment and ran down to his car. To save time he drove as close as he could to the cabin, taking back roads through the mountain range until he could go no further by vehicle.

He pulled off at a trailhead, parked the car, and ran about a half a mile before shifting in the camouflage of the trees, just in case anyone was on the trail. Picking his clothes up in his mouth, but leaving his boots where they were, he took off running.

Twenty minutes later Cedric was at the cabin. He dropped his clothes on the porch, leaving them there as he circled the perimeter, ensuring he smelled no intruders before going back to the door. Lifting one large paw he scratched at the wood.

It was Ryanne who opened the door. Stepping back out of the way, she made room for him to come in.

He immediately found the princess. She was sitting on the edge of the bed, her head high and her hands folded demurely in her lap. He did not approach her, unsure of what she would do if he did.

Ryanne gave him a small smile and turned to her sister. "We will continue this conversation later," she said.

Duana gave her a nod. "Yes. I'd like that…sister."

"I'm going to go get her some things," Ryanne told Cedric. "I'll be back in a couple of hours."

Tearing his gaze from his princess, he acknowledged what she'd told him. He would stay here and guard Duana.

When Ryanne left, he padded out onto the small porch and watched her until she took off through the trees. Then he came back inside, nosing the door shut behind him. Running his eyes over Duana to make sure she seemed okay with him being there, he huffed out a breath and sat by the door.

After a few moments, she sighed heavily and stood up from the bed. Eyes on the floor, she began to pace. "If you've come here with some misguided male idea that I need to be guarded, there's no need," she told him. "I am assured that this place has been mystically protected and the prince will not find me here. Nor am I about to go anywhere." She stopped walking. Slowly and methodically, her eyes ran over his large form. "So, this is the wolf that killed my brother." It wasn't said in a hateful way, it was just more of an observation. "It's actually quite impressive," she continued. "It's not easy to take down a faerie as powerful as my brother was. Especially not single-handedly." She paused, her head tilting in thought. "Although, from what you told me, he must have been severely injured by the time you came upon him."

Cedric dipped his head, confirming the thoughts she voiced aloud.

The princess continued her pacing. Back and forth and back and forth. It wasn't a very large room, but still she made a regal figure, even as beaten down as she was. Her chin held high, she walked with a natural grace that stemmed from her breeding.

It reminded Cedric of the first time he'd seen her, sitting in that ridiculous throne next to her father, him in his much larger and more obnoxious chair. She had caught his eye right away. And she had paced before him much like she was doing now, her heels clicking on the floor and her scent filling his nose, the soft curves of her body drawing his eyes. And he'd let them wander aplenty.

He remembered thinking to himself then how she was exquisite in a dress of emerald green, her smoky voice drifting along his senses, lighting him up from the inside out. She had affected him like no other female ever had.

But what he'd felt that day had nothing on what she was doing to him now. A lady in red...just like the song.

"Would you please change back and talk to me? I can't stand you just sitting there staring at me."

At her command, Cedric stood and made to go outside. It would be a risk. If anything happened, he would lose precious minutes shifting back to protect her. However, he could refuse her nothing.

"No," she told him. "Do it here. I want to see."

He shook his head once. Watching a werewolf shift back to their human form was not a pretty sight.

She heaved a sigh. "If you're going to be shy about it, I'll turn around," she told him. "But t if you leave this cabin, you'll be outside of the wards. Isn't that so?"

She had a point. Cedric waited for her to turn around and then he began to shift back. He made no noise other than a grunt or two as his bones broke and his muscles tore, only to reknit and rejoin back into his human form. When he was done, he opened the cabin door and stepped out onto the porch, picking up his shirt and pants and bringing them inside. Quickly, he pulled on his jeans and shut the door.

The princess turned back around. Her eyes traveled leisurely over his bare chest, setting his skin afire as they made their way down to his unfastened jeans. Quickly, dipping down to his bare feet and back.

The heat that rose within him was much like he felt right before his wolf came out. His heart tried to punch its way out of his chest. His blood raced, hot and quick through his veins, pushed on by the colors flashing in her eyes.

"You really are a beautiful beast of a man," she said in a distracted voice, almost like she hadn't meant to say it loud.

"I'm glad ye came tae me," he told her.

"I can't forgive you for what you did to my brother."

"I ken that, but I'm still glad ye came tae me. I will protect ye with my life, Duana."

Suddenly the colors in her eyes turned wavy, shining with tears. "Why?" she asked. "I've been nothing but horrible to you."

"No," he said, shaking his head. "Ye have been honest and ye have been scared. And ye were trying tae protect yerself."

She dropped her eyes, staring down at the floor as she wiped the tears from her cheeks. "I don't know why I'm being so emotional."

Dropping his shirt on a small table by the door, Cedric took a step closer. "I ken ye can no' forgive me for what I did," he told her. "And I ken ye can no' forget. But I can no' help but hope, someday, ye will find it in yerself tae realize I did no' do what I did with any intent tae hurt ye. And perhaps one day, kitten, ye will feel safe enough with me tae retract yer claws."

One side of her mouth lifted in a self-depreciating smile. "I feel safer with you than I do my own father," she told him. "How fucked up is that?"

"Can we stop with the games now?" he asked her, taking another step closer. "I want tae hold ye in my arms." Another step. "I want tae protect ye and take care o' ye. I want tae sit next tae ye at night and watch stupid shows on Netflix. I want ye tae lead yer people by my side. I want ye tae be my partner. In life. In love. In everything."

"I can't," she whispered.

"Why no'? Tell me ye dinna feel the way I feel," he dared her. "Tell me ye dinna want those things, tae."

A single tear spilled over onto her cheek. "I can't," she whispered.

At her simple confession, Cedric began to shake. He stepped closer until she had to tilt her head back to look up at him. "Touch me," he pleaded. "Touch me and show me it was no' just a dream. I ken it was no' just a dream. And yet, I can no' get myself tae truly believe it. Please, kitten. Touch me."

With a hand that visibly trembled, she ran her fingertips through the hair on his chest, and his entire body shuttered as he released a breath, a breath he hadn't realized he'd been holding, only to inhale sharply when she dragged her nails down over his abs.

That intriguing scent he so loved rose between heavily them, the heavy musk of her desire mixing with the fresh, cool smell of Snowdrops. A low growl rose from his chest before he could stop it, and her eyes flashed up to his. Declarations of his love and admiration rose to his lips, but Cedric clamped his mouth shut. For somehow, he knew if he said anything more, he would break the spell between them.

Instead, he lowered his head and caught her lips with his.

Och, the taste of her filled his mouth as the feel of her filled his arms. Duana's hands slid up his chest to grip his shoulders, hanging on like he was her rock in the middle of a storm. The material of her dress was silky beneath his palms, sliding along her skin effortlessly as he slid it up over her sweet arse. She wore nothing but a slip of lace beneath. He desperately wanted to see what color they were.

Cedric growled deep, images of her walking across the flood in nothing but her lace panties and high heels flashing through his mind. "I want tae rip this dress off o' ye," he confessed against her lips. "But then I would no' be able tae see ye in it ever again." He kissed her again, hard, before tearing his mouth away. "And the thought o' that breaks my fookin' heart."

Releasing her dress before he lost control and did exactly that, he took her wee face between his palms and pressed his lips to her cheeks, her eyes, her nose, before coming back to her sweet mouth. As he kissed her, he breathed her into his lungs, absorbing her scent until there was nothing more but the smell of her...the taste of her...the feel of her against his body.

He kissed her until she was pressing against him, as desperate for him as he was for her. When he felt her hands at the opening of his jeans, he nearly yelled out, his cock swelling for her until all he could think of was being inside of her.

Cedric tore himself away from her, dropping his arms and stepping back. "Take off the dress," he ordered.

Duana trembled before him, sucking in breaths through her parted lips, red and swollen from his kisses. All the colors of the rainbow blazed in her eyes as she stared up at him.

"Take off the dress," he repeated. "Now. Or I'm going tae rip it from yer body. And then I will have tae kill the next person who shows up here for seeing ye in a way that is only for me."

She inhaled sharply.

"Ye are mine, Duana. Dinna argue with me aboot it," he ordered when she opened her mouth to do just that. "Now take off the FOOKIN' dress."

With hands that shook, she reached up to the back of her neck and unzipped the small zipper, then tugged the hemline up over her hips, her belly, her breasts, and finally up and over her head. Looking around, she stepped to the side and let it float down to land on the table on top of his shirt.

His princess stood before him in nothing but red lace and black heels.

"Take off the bra."

She paused only for a moment before she undid the front hook, peeling back the lace until her breasts tumbled out of the cups. They swayed, loose and gorgeous as she added her bra to the pile of clothes.

Entranced, Cedric ran his eyes over her body. She didn't cower or try to hide herself, but stood proud and tall.

Her chin lifted as her eyes bore into his.

A challenge.

Cedric smiled in anticipation. "Walk tae the bed." He tugged his jeans off, his eyes never leaving her shapely legs and arse as she did what he said. The view was even better than he'd imagined. He had been right all those months ago. His princess was exquisite. Perfect.

Taking himself in his hand, he waited until she stopped before joining her. Duana turned, studying him as he approached, much as he had her, and by the way her colorful eyes lit up, she also liked what he saw.

However, when he got to her, and she immediately reached

out to touch him, Cedric groaned, making no move to stop her as she explored him.

And when her wee hands wrapped greedily around his cock, he ground his teeth together but could not repress the moan that left him. "Aye, lass," he encouraged her.

"I want to taste you," she told him.

Cedric grabbed her wrists, pulling her hands away. He'd nearly come just hearing the words leave her sweet lips. "I could no' take it. No' right now. Ye dinna ken what ye do tae me, kitten."

Her eyes shone with her newfound power.

"Dinna look at me like that, or I'll bend ye over my knee and spank the sweet flesh o' yer arse until ye can no' sit down without thinking o' me." He smiled to soften the threat. However, he totally meant it.

And by the way his princess's eyes lit up as she sucked in a breath, she was as excited as he was by the thought.

Cedric cupped her jaw, rubbing his thumb over her plump bottom lip. "But right now, I just want tae love ye."

Her lips curved up into a soft smile, and unable to resist the invitation, he took her mouth with his and lowered her onto the bed. Raising up, he gave in to his desire and tore the last piece of lace from her, dropping the ruined underwear beside the bed.

Leaving the heels on her feet, he ran his hands up her thighs, spreading them. She opened for him, her sex glistening in the soft light of the cabin. Cedric ran his thumb up her center, finding the hard nub and teasing it. He watched as her eyes closed and her hips moved, mimicking his movements. Her breasts rose and fell and her lips parted, her breath leaving her on a moan.

When her hands fisted in the blankets, he slid his thumb down, sliding inside of her. She was tight and hot and wet, and it was all he could do not to slide inside and take his pleasure.

But he wanted to watch her first.

She moved her hips restlessly, and he pulled out his thumb and went back to her clit. His free hand gripped her hip, holding her still as his thumb slid around the hard nub, faster and faster, until her back arched and she cried out his name.

She was still coming when he moved over her. With one hard stroke, he pushed inside. Her body convulsing around him, Cedric slid one hand beneath her arse, lifting her hips so he could go deeper. He took her fast and hard, his lips on hers, swallowing her cries as he thrust deep, his hips slamming into her.

Burying his face in her neck, Cedric pumped his hips faster. Harder. Each breath burning in his lungs and his heart pounding in his chest, his own pleasure barreled down on him like a freight train, taking over his body. Cedric sank his teeth into the muscle between her neck and shoulder as his orgasm hit him, pulling her body up into his so tightly he didn't know where he ended and she began. It tore through him, splintering his soul and fracturing his heart until he knew he would never be whole again without her.

When he could breathe again, Cedric brushed her hair from her face, slid his fingers beneath her chin, and tilted her face up to his. He kissed her forehead, her nose, and finally her sweet lips. "I meant everything I said before," he told her. "I want ye tae stay with me, kitten."

"I…"

He covered her mouth with his hand. "Dinna say it," he told her. "Dinna say ye can no'. For I could no' live without ye now."

He removed his hand and pressed his forehead to hers. "Princess…please. Ye are mine. And I am yours. We need tae be together. Do ye no' feel it?"

She gave him a sad smile, running her fingers through his ponytail. "The prince will find me, Cedric," she said. "Eventually, he will. He will find me, and he will kill me. And when he finds out my sister is alive, he will kill her, too."

Cedric started to shake his head.

"You know it's true," she told him. "And then he will send someone for you. Just like he killed my brother."

His chest tightened as tingles ran up his arms. Not because he was afraid of dying. But because this was the first time she did not blame him for her brother's death. Yet, even so, it was something he would atone for the rest of his life. "I will keep ye safe," he told her. "The prince will no' get tae ye."

"How will you stop him all by yourself?" she asked. "I can't even stop him."

"I am no' going tae stop him by myself," he told her. "We are going tae stop him. Ye, me, Keelin and Ryanne, along with the pack. We will stop him. And we will have our life together. Ye just have tae trust me. Do ye trust me, Duana?"

She stared at him for such a long time, his blood began to chill.

"I do," she told him.

Cedric closed his eyes, relief making him lightheaded. "Thank ye," he whispered.

Pushing on his shoulders, she rolled him over on the bed and climbed on top of him, straddling his hips. "But before we go conquer the faerie prince, I would like to do this one more time," she said. "Just in case I don't ever get to do it again."

"Aye," he told her. "That sounds like a grand plan."

CHAPTER 15

L ucian caught the ball in his hands, and grinned at his son. "Excellent toss!"

There was no doubt in his mind now that Finn was his son by blood, and it completely flabbergasted him that he had never seen it before.

Actually, he did know how he'd never noticed. Because he had been too caught up in his own self-perceived problems and his anger at everyone in the world for things he had only brought on himself.

Above the child's giggles and shouts for him to throw the ball back, Lucian caught a familiar voice, one that did not belong in this camp. Tossing the ball back to Finn, he held his finger over his lips, telling him to be quiet, and snuck around the corner of the closest tent. He had no worries that his son would not do what he'd told him. Shifter children were raised to obey their elders from the time they were bairns. The pack's lives depended on it.

Peering around the side, his suspicions were confirmed. The fookin' faerie prince was in the camp.

Lucian swiftly hid behind the tent. He could not find him there.

Finn ran up to him. "Are we playing a new game Uncle Lucian?" he whispered.

"No," he told him. "I'm sorry, lad, but I have tae go. I'll be back verra soon," he told him.

"Ye promise?"

"Aye, I promise. Now go find yer ma." He watched as the lad walked off to do as he'd been told.

Checking that the prince hadn't wandered away, Lucian took off in the opposite direction. Once he hit the cover of the woods, he shifted and ran full out to his truck. Shifting back, he climbed in completely nude and sped all the way home. When he arrived at the apartments, he reached into the back-seat to grab the blanket Keelin kept in the truck, but it wasn't there.

Och, aye. The females would just have to get over it.

Once inside, he ran straight to Cedric's apartment and pounded repeatedly on the door. There was no answer, so he went up to Marc's apartment.

Bronaugh cracked the door, opening it wider when she saw him standing there in nothing but his skin. At the sight of her ghastly appearance his upper lip lifted, exposing his canines as he snarled. But he made no move to attack her. No matter the threat he perceived her to be, she was Marc's mate. And although he and Marc had never gotten along very well. He would never do anything to hurt him, not on purpose. Not without cause.

He held her glowing red eyes with his own. "Where is

Marc?"

Lowering her lids and hiding her eyes, she stepped back and let him in the apartment.

"Och, man, what are ye doing running around like that in front of my Bronaugh? Have ye no decency?"

"Where is Cedric?" Lucian asked. "I have tae speak tae him. It's verra important." He kept Bronaugh in his line of vision. He didn't trust her. She was going dark, just like he knew she would. But what he really wanted to know was, how long has it been happening?

Her appearance had shocked him when she first walked into Cedric's apartment the day before, and she looked even worse today.

"Is he no' back yet?" Marc asked. "Last I ken he went tae the cabin tae check on the princess. He must still be there."

"I need tae speak tae him," Lucian said. "It's important."

"Why dinna ye just text him?"

"I left my phone...somewhere," he finished lamely.

"I'll text him," Marc said.

Lucian was happy he didn't question him further. "I'll go get dressed and meet ye at his apartment." He paused on his way out. "Everyone should be there."

Thirty minutes later, Lucian and Keelin, Marc and Bronaugh, Brock and Heather, and Duncan and Ryanne were all standing outside Cedric's apartment when he walked up. "What is it? What's happened?" Punching in the code on his door, he let them all into the apartment.

Once they all got inside, the girls took a seat in the living room, leaving room for Brock to sit next to Heather on the couch as he couldn't stand to have her out of his reach unless he had to. The rest of them stood in a circle between the furniture.

"What's the emergency?" Cedric asked.

"The prince is at Thomas's camp," Lucian told him. "They are planning an attack."

"An attack on who?" Brock asked.

"An attack on us," Lucian told him. "All o' us." His eyes touched on each of them, even the females. "He's done waiting. He's done playing games. I heard him telling Thomas that he had found a way tae open the portal and release the things inside."

Bronaugh shot him a dirty look, which he ignored.

Then they all started talking at once until Marc held up his hand, calling for quiet. Brows drawn together over his dark eyes, he narrowed them at Lucian. "How did ye happen tae overhear this?"

Lucian threw his shoulders back. "Because I was at Thomas's camp."

"What?" Keelin looked up at him in surprise.

"Ye ken where Thomas's camp is?" Marc said.

"Aye, I do."

"You've known all this time?" Brock asked him.

"And ye haven't told us," Marc added.

"No, I can no'," Lucian said.

Marc took a threatening step toward him, his upper lip lifted in a snarl, baring his canines. "I told Cedric we should never have trusted ye," he told him. "Yer a traitor tae our pack."

Keelin jumped up. "You don't know what you're talking about, Marc!"

Lucian pulled her out from between the two wolves and put her behind him. "I am no' a traitor," Lucian told him.

"Then why can ye no' tell us where the camp is?"

"Because my bairn is there," he said. "My son. And I swore I would no' tell anyone where they are. If I do, Thomas will kill him."

"No, he will no'," Marc said.

"Aye, he will. And for that reason, and that reason alone, I can no' tell ye where Thomas's camp is."

Marc took a threatening step toward him, but Cedric appeared between the two. He pushed Marc away. "We dinna have time for this," he growled. "Ye two can work out yer stuff later. Right now, we need tae prepare."

Cedric turned to Lucian and laid his hands on his shoulders. "Lucian, ye have tae trust me. Now more than ever. Ye must tell us where Thomas's camp is if we want tae prevent our pack from being slaughtered."

"With all due respect, Cedric, I can no'."

By the tense set of his jaw and shoulders, Cedric knew Lucian would not be moved. He could call out his alpha and force him to tell him. But it was important to Cedric that he not do that. He and Lucian had always had a touchy relationship, although it had gotten better since he'd mated with Keelin. But the tension was still there, and if they were going to stop the prince, he needed his full trust and cooperation.

He squeezed his shoulders. "Lucian, I swear tae ye, we will no' hurt your child. We will get him out."

"How will ye do that?" Lucian asked, his expression guarded.

"Ye got in there without them noticing, did ye not?" Duncan said.

"Aye," Lucian told him.

"Well, how did ye do it?"

"I just walked in," Lucian said. "And let them see me. And I swore tae Thomas that if he would let me spend time with Finn, that I would tell no' anyone where their camp is. I can no' break that promise."

"Not even for the life of your own pack?"

Lucian's gaze clashed with Cedric's.

"Your own mate?"

Lucian stared at him long and hard. But in the end, he knew he didn't have a choice. Not without risking his pack. Not without risking Keelin. "Ye have tae promise me we will get Finn out," he bit out. "Ye have tae swear it!"

"Aye, I swear it," Cedric told him.

"And his mother, Sara," Lucian said. "She needs tae come tae, I dinna want him tae lose his ma."

"What about Sara's mate?" Brock asked him.

"I dinna give a fook about him. He can choose his own destiny. But I want Sara and Finn out and safely away before anything happens."

"Ye have my word," Cedric told him. "As your alpha. I will go in and I will get them personally."

"No." Lucien shook his head. "Let me do it. My scent is familiar in the camp and will no' raise an alarm. I can get in and out without anybody noticing I'm there."

"We'll do it tonight," Cedric said.

Lucian hesitated for a moment, and then he gave him a nod. "Thank ye," he told him.

Cedric waved away his gratitude. "'Tis yer son. O' course we will get him out. We would not want him in any danger in any way. So, tonight, he will come here, where he'll be safe."

"Maybe that's no' such a good idea," Marc said.

Lucian growled deep in his throat and leaned toward him.

Marc held up a hand. "I only meant bringing him back here. I dinna ken it would be safe."

"Aye, yer right," Cedric told him. "We can take him tae the cabin. He can stay with the princess."

"No, I do no' trust her," Lucian told him.

"I do," Cedric said. "She does no' want tae hurt her people. She wants tae save them. And she would no' hurt a child or his mother, either."

The wolves exchanged disbelieving glances.

"That's what she's been doing all this time," Cedric said. "She's trying tae come up with a cure so when the prince opens the portal and releases her people, she'll be able tae cure them as the addiction hits, before they can run amok in this world and destroy everything."

"And did she find a cure?" Duncan asked.

"No' yet," Cedric said.

"So, our only other option is to stop the prince before he can open the portal."

"Aye," Cedric said to Brock.

"All right then," Duncan said. "Let's go find us a prince."

"But first," Cedric said, turning back to Lucian. "We go get the boy and his mother. We get them safe."

"Tonight?" Lucian confirmed.

"Aye. Tonight," Cedric said.

CHAPTER 16

Duana paced the small room of the cabin. She hadn't seen Cedric for three days. Although he did send Marc —was that his name?—with some food and water and extra clothes, and with the order for her to stay where she was.

"Where is Cedric? I need to speak to him."

"He'll be along when he can," he'd told her just before he'd turned to leave.

Duana rushed up behind him and grabbed his arm. "Is he safe?" she'd asked. "Just…just tell me that he's safe."

The wolf had cocked his head, looking at her strangely. "Aye, he's fine," he'd finally told her. "He's the alpha." Then he'd left her alone again.

That had been days ago. But Duana had done as he'd asked and stayed inside the cabin. However, she was beginning to get quite antsy. Something was going on. She could sense it. She needed to know what was happening. Needed to know what her father was up to, because she would bet her life he was not sitting in their little house, mourning her loss.

Something creaked behind her and Duana spun around.

The alpha was coming through the doorway. Ducking his head, he stepped over the threshold.

Despite the other wolf's reassurances, relief such as she had never known flooded through her, making her momentarily lightheaded, and she rushed into his arms without thinking.

"Hey, hey," he said gently as she crashed into him. He wrapped her up in his powerful embrace. "It's okay," he told her. "It's okay."

She allowed herself to cling to him for a few more moments before she stepped back, but she kept a firm grip on his arms. Taking a deep breath, she pulled her composure around her. "I was concerned about you," she told him.

"Aye," he said with a grin. "I can see that." He touched her cheek, his white-blue eyes wandering over her face. "I brought ye a few things." Taking both of her hands in his, he kissed her knuckles before stepping back outside. He leaned over and picked something up off the porch, bringing it in to her.

He handed Duana a book, a few magazines, and some more food before ducking back out again. When he came back in, he had a bucket of ice that held a bottle of wine. The same wine they'd had on their first picnic together. "If you're trying to get me drunk, it won't work," she told him with a small smile. "Alcohol affects me about as much as it affects you." She thought about it for a second. "Perhaps slightly more than it affects you. But only slightly."

Cedric's deep laughter filled the cabin as he set the bucket on the little table by the door, easing the anxiety that had been riding her for days. "I just thought ye might like something besides water tae drink," he told her. "And some reading material." He took the book from her arms and held it up. It had a bare-chested man on the front of it. "It's a romance." He shrugged. "Heather says it's really good."

Duana eyed the thick tome dubiously. Not because of the material—she rather enjoyed reading romances—but because of the implications. "How long exactly do you expect me to stay here locked up in this cabin?"

The smile fell from Cedric's face as the hand holding the book drifted back down to his side. He set it on the table, then took the food into the kitchen and put it in the small fridge. "Until it's safe," he told her. "Until yer life is no longer in danger."

"My life will be in danger as long as the prince lives," she said.

Closing the door, he came back over to her. "I ken that. And that's why ye have tae stay here until we can get rid o' him."

"And how do you propose to do that?" she asked him. "Do you have a plan?"

"We're working on it," he told her.

Duana caught his eyes with hers, begging him to understand. "You can do nothing against the faerie prince, Cedric. He is more powerful than any of you know."

"We have the other lasses tae help us," he said.

But she shook her head. "All of them together do not have one fifth of his powers," she said.

"We have Keelin. She is The Key."

"That is her only power."

"We'll get him inside the portal before she closes it. It will have tae work," he insisted at her look of disbelief. "We will trick him somehow."

Duana laughed. "He's not as crazy as he lets you all think, you know."

"Aye, I had my suspicions," he told her seriously.

"Don't get me wrong," she said. "He is crazy. But not when it comes to his position of power. On that, I have recently discovered, he is ruthless."

Cedric stepped forward and took her face in large hands, forcing her to look up at him. "I will make this world safe for ye," he told her. "This I swear. I swear it on my very life."

"That's what I'm worried about," she told him. "It may be your life that you sacrifice."

Leaning down, he gave her a tender kiss. "I wish I could stay longer, but I need tae get back."

She grabbed his hand. "Cedric."

"Aye?"

"You can't go after the prince alone. Take me with you."

"He is yer father, Duana."

"I know. Cedric, do not leave me here in the dark with nothing to do but pace these damn floors."

He pressed his lips together, and she could tell by the look on his stubborn, handsome face that he wasn't going to listen to her. But then he sighed. "We're going after Thomas's camp tonight, no' yer father. Lucian overheard the prince while he was there. He said he was done waiting and he had found a way tae open the portal without Keelin."

Duana backed away from his touch. It distracted her too much. She couldn't think. "That's impossible," she said. There is no way to open the portal without The Key."

Cedric ran his hands over his head, smoothing back his ponytail. "I dinna think so either. But that's what he overheard."

"So, you're going to war with another pack?"

"Aye," he said. "But dinna fash yerself, kitten. We're

bringing back up. That's why I haven't been here. It took a few days to get the other packs together. And that's another reason why ye need tae stay inside. I can no' always be there if ye run across any rogue wolves."

"How many are here?" she asked.

"The full Oregon pack, the full Idaho pack and the Vancouver pack."

"Will it be enough?" she asked.

"Aye," he assured her. "Lucian said Thomas only has aboot fifty tae seventy wolves total. A third of them are females and bairns. Some o' the females will fight, but no' all."

"How does Lucian know all of this? Why was he in Thomas's camp?"

"He had his reasons," Cedric told her. "But they are no' my reasons tae tell." He smiled at her look of frustration. "Ye will see soon enough."

"What does that mean?"

"It means I'll be back, and I'll be bringing someone with me. Someone verra important to Lucian."

"I thought Lucian was mated to Keelin?"

"Aye, he is." But instead of giving her more information, Cedric just smiled and planted a sound kiss on her mouth. "I'll be back. I swear it tae ye. Do no' leave this cabin." He turned to leave, but paused with his hand on the door. "If anything happens tae me, Heather or one o' the other lasses will be here tae get ye away where ye can be safe."

A twinge of fear shot through her. "You said you had enough wolves."

He didn't say anything, but his eerie eyes roamed over her face and body, like he was trying to memorize every inch of her.

Oh, hell no. He was not leaving her here to worry while he was out there fighting. "I want to come with you."

"Absolutely no'."

"I can help you. Please, let me help you." She knew she was begging; she could hear the desperate plea in her own voice. But she was suddenly terrified that she would never see him again.

His face hardened as she argued with him, but then he stopped and took a breath. "I will no' risk yer life, princess. It's too important tae me."

"But you'll risk your own," she spat.

He grinned at her show of temper. "Och, kitten. Do ye no' have any faith in me?"

She stared at him, refusing to answer that asinine question.

Cedric winked. "I'll see ye soon. I promise." With one last look at her, he was out the door.

Duana rushed to the doorway, but he was already gone.

After he left, she went back to pacing, trying to warm the ice in her veins. He was lying to her. Or at the very least not telling her everything. She could feel it all the way to her bones.

Picking up the book, she flung it across the room. It hit the opposite wall with a satisfying thud and slid to the floor, landing face down on the floor, a few of the pages bent beneath it.

She couldn't stay in this cabin a minute longer. If she did, she would come out of her skin. Did he actually expect her to sit and...and...read a book while he was out there getting himself killed?

Her mind began to work. There had to be something she

could do. She was the only one who could get close to the prince without him being suspicious…

Duana suddenly stopped and her eyes fell on the bottle of wine. She knew what she had to do. And it was very likely her father would kill her the moment he saw her face, but it was a risk she had to take.

It was the only way to save the wolf who had stolen her heart.

Picking up the book, she laid it open on the bed, then found a pen in a drawer in the kitchen.

CHAPTER 17

Duana figured her chances would be better if she knocked on the front door where people could see her rather than just walk into the house. It would at least give her a few seconds to talk her father into not killing her as soon as he set eyes on her, enough time to explain why she was there and hopefully win him over onto her side.

Bottle of his favorite wine in hand, she took a deep breath, and knocked. She knew she didn't need to announce herself; he would know she was there from the moment she'd arrived.

For a minute, she thought perhaps he wasn't home. But that couldn't be. She felt him there just as clearly as he felt her. They were blood after all. Duana rolled her eyes when she realized what he was doing. He was making her wait. A child's way to punish her for turning against him. So, she stood patiently. She didn't fidget. She didn't look away. She just stood and waited.

Sure enough, after the allotted amount of time had passed, he opened the door. Her father did not smile at her or greet her in any way, he just tilted his head to the side and stared at her, his expression glowing with a sense of pride that she had had the balls to show up at his door. She knew this because she would have felt the same way if the roles had been reversed.

Duana held out the bottle of wine. "I've brought a peace offering," she said. "All I ask is that you give me a few minutes to explain to you why I'm here. And then you can do whatever you feel you must." She stuck the wine in his face to make him look at it.

"It's going to take a lot more than my favorite wine to talk me into letting you back into the fold," he said.

She noticed he had a hard time saying "not murdering you" outright, and she took that as a good sign. "Five minutes," she said. "That's all. I have news that you might find important to your cause."

"And you hope to win my favor by telling me this news?"

"Yes," she told him honestly. "Of course. I really don't want to die, father. And I think you will see that I've thought about things, and I'm on your side."

Her father studied her, glanced at the wine, and finally stepped back with a nod to wave her inside.

"Your word," she told him. "I need your word that you're not going to zap me down the moment you close the door."

With an exaggerated roll of his eyes and a great sigh of grievance, he nodded. "Yes, yes, fine. I give you my word." "Five minutes," Duana reminded him.

"Yes," he agreed. "Five minutes."

She didn't really believe him, but what choice did she have? So, she stepped inside the house. The first thing she noticed was that he hadn't fixed anything from her temper tantrum.

"I'll get some glasses and you can tell me what it is that's so important you think it is worth your life," her father said cheerfully before he bounced off into the kitchen to grab a few wine glasses.

Taking a deep breath, Duana followed him. Luckily, there was still a part of the counter near the stove that was still intact, and she walked over there and set the bottle down. Grabbing the corkscrew out of the drawer, she poured them both glass of wine, handing her father his. "I came here to offer up a truce," she told him.

He swished the wine in his glass, holding it to the light. "Go on," he said. Pulling an old fashioned timepiece out of his pocket, he checked the time. "The clock is ticking, my dear." He stuck his nose in the glass and then took a sip, holding the wine in his mouth for a moment. "Perfect," he sighed.

"I will give you the information I have IF you agree to my terms," she told him.

"And what are those terms, my dear?"

"I will sign a royal decree that I will not come after your crown or your position, if you allow me to try to save at least some of my people." She was not ready to save anyone. Though her team had assured her not forty minutes ago they were working tirelessly, they had yet to come up with anything that didn't kill their subjects.

Duana had never been so glad to hear anything in her life.

Her father sipped his wine and gave her a bored sigh. "You can do with the people what you will."

Because he doesn't believe I can cure them.

His eyes never left her face, and Duana was careful, very, very careful, not to show one inkling of emotion. He took a sip of his wine. "And what of your beau?" he asked.

"First of all," she said. "He's not my beau. How you ever

thought I would mate with one such as him I have no idea. He's gruff, he's uncouth. He's...gruff. And he doesn't even know how to dress for dinner. Although he did keep me well fed for the last few weeks." The prince knew her penchant for food, and so it would be easily believable that this was a valid reason for her to continue seeing the alpha wolf.

He eyed her warily. "What's in this for you? Other than trying to save your people, which is such a lost cause. What if you can't save them?"

"Then at least I will have saved myself," she said.

The prince made a big show of thinking over her offer. Standing up, he held his hands behind him and paced back and forth, stepping gracefully over broken pieces of chairs and tiles.

Finally, he came to a stop directly in front of her. "All right," he said. "I agree." Waving his hand in the air, purple sparkles appeared at his fingertips. They spun in and out of each other, until they formed the shape of a sheet of paper. Translucent and glittery, it hovered in the air. Words appeared on the decree as the prince spoke them. "I, Princess Duana of the *an olc*, hereby swear upon my life that I will never covet the throne of Prince Nada, nor any of his power. Instead, I will go off to live a lonely and boring existence trying unsuccessfully to cure the addiction he created of which there is no cure. However, I will agree to this anyway. And in return, the prince, my father, will allow me to live in seclusion alone and with no one else, but I will be alive." With a flourish, he signed his name - Prince Nada of the *na maithe* and *an olc*.

With another wave of his hand, the translucent paper floated down to the counter, where it grew more and more opaque. Snapping his fingers, a pen appeared out of thin air.

He Marced where she should sign with an "X", then handed it to Duana. "Here you are, dear."

She signed her name. As soon as she'd finished, the decree rolled itself and appeared in the prince's hand. Carefully, he tucked it into the inside breast pocket of his jacket. "Now," he said. "Tell me what you know."

She swirled her untouched glass of wine. "Cedric and his pack are aware of your plans," she told him. "You were over-heard at Thomas's camp. They are, at this moment, on their way to wage war against the other pack."

Her father threw his head back and laughed. "It's perfect!" he said. He took a great gulp of his wine, finishing it off, and poured himself another glass. "A toast!" he called.

"A toast for what?" she asked cooly.

"For my plans going exactly as planned." He clicked his glass to hers, then took a drink. The prince frowned, took another sip of his wine, and clicked his tongue. His eyes looked off to the side. "Where did you say you got this wine? It does taste a bit off."

Duana lowered her glass without taking a drink. She didn't say anything. She couldn't.

She had just murdered her father.

She watched as the realization ghosted across his face. Faintly at first, and then growing stronger and more convinced. Like a fog rolling in from the sea. "What have you done?" he asked her quietly. His voice was not raised. There was no injustice or anger in his tone, but something more like awe.

Duana was surprised by the sudden feel of moisture on her cheeks. The image of her father wavered before her eyes, like she was looking at them through a waterfall. "I'm sorry," she told him. "I truly am. But you left me no other choice."

Her father smiled at her. His eyes filled with pride. "You are just like me. You would do anything for your people, just as I would. Do you see?"

"The only difference is the wolves are now also my people. And I will not do anything that will bring them any harm."

"So, my plan did work." A grin lit up his face, only to fall again. "Don't tell me you care about the humans, too?"

Duana waved away his words. "Don't be ridiculous. However, Cedric cares about them. And I must respect his feelings."

Pure delight crossed his features, even as his mouth twisted with the first pain of the herbs. "I was right," he said. "You two are the perfect match. It's a shame he won't be able to enjoy it much longer."

Duana looked up sharply. "What do you mean?" Fear wound its way through her. Had she missed something? Was it all a trap? Had he outsmarted her? It wouldn't be the first time, nor would it be the last if he somehow survived. But no, she couldn't think like that. He would not survive. There was no way. Even when as powerful as he was, he could not counteract what was happening inside of him. "You must be delirious," she told him. "There's nothing stopping Cedric and I from being together."

"There is one thing," he told her. "You're here because you don't want me releasing the Dark Fae before your boyfriend can seal the portal. Is that correct?"

Duana narrowed her eyes at him. "Where exactly are you going with this?"

He took a step toward her, but made no other threatening

moves, so she held her ground. Bending at the waist, he leaned in toward her. "That means, my dear, that we still have time."

"Time for what?" she gritted out.

Pain drew ugly lines in his still handsome face. "It means…" He stopped, fighting for breath. "We still have time to get there first."

Before she could fully comprehend his words, his hands shot out and grabbed her around the wrist and Duana found herself tumbling through time. The wind whipped around her ears, tearing the clothes from her body as they tumbled into another dimension, back to her world. The world the wolves were about to seal closed. And if they succeeded in sealing the portal, they would be locking her in here forever.

CHAPTER 18

When Cedric arrived back at the cabin, everyone was already gathered there: Brock, Heather, Marc, Bronaugh Lucian, Keelin. Even Duncan and Ryanne.

And Sara and Finn.

The back of his left shoulder burned from a particularly bad bite, but otherwise, he'd made it through the fight okay. As had the rest of the pack.

Mostly thanks to the lasses, all of whom were staring at him with the most innocent expressions, despite breaking his direct order to stay far away from the melee.

"Are ye sure this is safe?" Lucien asked, his arm wrapped protectively around Keelin.

"It's warded by the witches," Cedric said. "'Tis the safest place I can think o'. And as Keelin explained it tae me, she can do this from anywhere."

"That's correct," Keelin said.

"And yer sure this will work?" Duncan asked.

"I'm no' sure about anything," Cedric told him. "But it's all we've got."

"We don't have the princess blood or magic," Keelin said. "But I think between myself, Ryanne, Bronaugh and Heather, we can take care of the magic part. But the blood...I'm not so sure."

"If we use mine and Duana's blood, I believe it will work," Ryanne said. "We're both his daughters. Between the two of us, it should be pure enough to lock the portal."

"Now we just have to talk Duana into doing it," Heather said.

"That's easier said than done." Cedric sighed. "She's no' ready for the portal tae be closed and I promised her I would give her time tae come up with a cure. But with the crazy prince going on as he is, time is running out."

"We have no choice," Keelin agreed. "We have to do this now."

"Aye. I hope I can convince her o' that."

"Well, there's only one way to find out," Brock said, opening the door to the cabin. He held it open wide, allowing Cedric to go through first.

He called out to her when he came into the cabin, expecting her to run to him as she had before. Or maybe she would want to portray a more royal demeanor with everyone there. But surely, she would be excited to see him.

However, it was eerily silent. "Duana!" he called. "Princess!" He peeked around into the kitchen. And then looked across the room. The door to the simple bath was open.

She wasn't there. For a moment, fear froze him where he stood. "Dammit, kitten. What are ye doing?"

Where is she?" Heather asked.

"I dinna ken," he responded. "But we need tae find her."

Ryanne caught Cedric's eye, hers were flashing colors. "You don't think…"

Cedric didn't know what to think. But he knew what he felt in his gut. "No. She would no' endanger us."

"But wouldn't she?" Bronaugh asked. "We all know she's near as crazy as he is."

Cedric cursed. "I'll take care o' this."

"I'll go with you," Marc told him. He held out his hand Bronaugh. "There's nothing for us tae do here. Heather and Brock can keep an eye on Sara and Finn."

"Wait." Ryanne stood by the bed. "Cedric. Look."

She handed him the novel he'd left for Duana. Some of the pages were bent at odd angles, but that isn't what he noticed first.

One sentence was written across the page…

I do trust you. Now you need to trust me. I cannot allow you to go after my father. Close the portal.

Cedric read what she'd written three times. She was going after the prince. Alone.

Dammit, kitten. Why did ye no' wait for me?

"Can ye close the portal without Duana?"

"Where is she?" Heather asked.

Ryanne searched Cedric's closed off expression. "She went after our father on her own, didn't she?" A grudging look of respect entered her brown eyes.

Cedric turned back to Keelin. "Can ye close the portal, lass?"

Keelin looked around at the other Fae. "I'm not sure. Maybe Ryanne's blood will be enough, but there's no way to know until we test it."

"Should we wait?" Ryanne asked her.

"Do we have time?" Cedric asked. "Can ye give me an hour...no...two hours, tae find the princess and bring her back here?"

Keelin cast a worried glance Cedric's way. "I don't think we do," she said. "I can feel the portal opening. I can feel the souls within. If we wait..." She shook her head. "No. The longer we wait, the more chance there is that some of them will get out. And I don't really know how long it will take me to close it." Her voice dropped to a whisper. "I've never done it before."

Tension tightening his jaw until it ached, Cedric gave her a nod. "Do what ye must," he told her. "I'll go get the princess, and we'll be back in plenty of time."

"What aboot the prince?" Sara spoke up from the corner of the room where she was huddled with her son.

All eyes turned to her.

She met them all, one by one. "The prince will kill ye," she stated matter of factly. "Ye dragged me away from my pack, killed my mate, killed my alpha and the gods only ken how many o' my friends. I need yer protection. Finn needs yer protection."

"And ye will it, Sara. I swear." He did not apologize for winning the fight with Thomas. It was the way of wolves. She would adapt. And maybe, in time, find a new mate. In the meantime, she and Finn were safe, and that was all that mattered.

"I need tae go find the princess. Hopefully, I'll get there in time, before she does something rash."

Keelin held her hand out to Ryanne. Ryanne took it, and they stepped into the center of the room.

The Key glanced back over her shoulder, meeting Cedric's

eyes. They exchanged a long look, and then she turned back to Ryanne and took a blade from her back pocket.

Brock and Lucian backed away to stand guard at the door, both wearing identical expressions of worry, although Lucian's gave more of an impression of anger.

"Dinna worry aboot me," Cedric told them quietly. "I'll be right back." He tried to give them his typical grin, but didn't quite get there. Marc and Bronaugh followed right behind him.

Once outside, they ran through the woods to where Cedric Cedric's car was parked. He was in the car and had the engine running before the other two arrived.

As Bronaugh slid in beside him, he said, "This would be a good time tae travel as the Fae do." He meant it as a joke. He wasn't expecting Bronaugh's answer.

"I could try," she said. "But I'm not guaranteeing we would end up in right the location."

Cedric glanced over at her as he navigated the rutted out road and made his way down the mountain. She didn't look well at all. Dark circles were heavy under her eyes. And her normally vibrant hair was limp and lackluster. The skin was pulled tight across her mouth. And her eyes were tired and haunting. "Are ye all right, lass?"

"I will be," she said, and a look of determination hardened her features.

"The prince has been calling his people," Marc told him. "And my Bronaugh has been fighting it off. This is why she's been acting the way she has."

Bronaugh glanced at him sharply.

"It's okay," Marc told her. "He kens."

"Hang in there," Cedric told her. "Tis almost over, lass."

They were halfway to Seattle when Bronaugh suddenly stiffened beside him and took a sharp breath.

"Bronaugh!" Panic laced Marc's voice. "What's wrong, lass?"

She didn't answer.

Cedric took his eyes off the road just long enough to check on her.

Her face was frozen in an expression of horror.

He was about to pull over when suddenly she inhaled a short, sharp breath, followed quickly by a few more. She began to visibly shake.

Marc pulled her into his lap. "Just breathe, lass. I'm here. Just breathe."

"Something has happened." Her frightened eyes were locked to Cedric's.

Clenching his jaw, he punched down on the gas. They made it to the prince's house in record time. Cedric barely remembered to put the car into park. Leaping out, he left the motor running and the door open as he ran to the house and kicked the door open.

His wolf prowled beneath the surface of the skin. "Duana!" he called. "Princess!"

"She's not here," Bronaugh said from behind him.

"Where the fuck is she?" Cedric yelled. He was barely holding on to his self-control. His wolf tearing at him, ready to protect its female with teeth and claw and blood, the only way it knew how.

But Cedric couldn't let it out. He had to keep his wits about him if he was going to find Duana. At least for the moment.

As if in a daze, Bronaugh walked slowly into the kitchen.

Cedric followed her, as did Marc. There was a bottle of wine on the counter and two broken wine glasses on the floor.

Cedric picked up the bottle and sniffed at the contents, quickly putting it down again. There was something wrong with that wine.

"Gods be damned," Bronaugh said. "She tried to kill him."

Marc was watching her closely, his own wolf rippling under his skin. "He's her father," he said in disbelief.

"And she tried to kill him," Bronaugh told him. "I think she may have succeeded."

"Then where the fuck is she?" Cedric growled.

Bronaugh closed her eyes and held up her hand to quiet the two wolves.

They obeyed her wish, waiting quietly as she did whatever it was she was doing.

When she opened her eyes, the kaleidoscope of colors within in were shiny with tears. "I think I know where they went."

CHAPTER 19

"Can ye take me there?" Cedric asked.

Bronaugh immediately shook her head. "I don't think I can do it," she told him. "Fighting off the prince's call has left me so drained. I'm weak. I don't know if I can do it," she cried. She grabbed onto Marc as though to anchor herself, her mesmerizing eyes searching his face. "I'll lose myself."

"You must," Cedric said, barely keeping a handle on his wolf. Threats that were totally unlike him on the tip of his tongue.

He took a deep breath and paced away, smoothing back his hair. It wasn't her fault. The lass was frightened. Threatening her would not get him anywhere.

When he came back to the kitchen, Marc had taken her face between his hands. "Bronaugh, my love. Ye ken ye can do this. Yer more powerful than ye think," he reminded her. "Remember at the rodeo. Ye saved my life after being shocked and beaten and dragged around a ring."

"But that was you," she told him.

179

"And this is me, tae," he told her. "This is me, tae. Because if ye don't help Cedric, he will have lost his mate."

She grabbed his hands and pulled them away from her face. "Is this true?" she asked. "The princess...that female is your mate?" Disgust dripped from her voice.

"Dinna judge him," Marc reprimanded her. "Many said the same aboot ye." Gently, he turned her face back toward him.

Cedric watched from the side, feeling awkward. Like an intruder. But hoping and praying he would get through to her. It was his only chance.

"Ye can do this. Ye have tae. Because if ye dinna, my alpha will die o' a broken heart. And without an alpha..." He let the sentence dangle, the pain on his face speaking for itself. "It would be like losing ye, lass. I could no' live through it."

Cedric thought he was exaggerating just a wee bit, but he didn't interrupt.

"What if I can't?" she said.

"All I'm asking is that ye try," he told her. "Just try. Please, lass. That's all I'm asking o' ye."

She took a deep breath, glancing woefully at the bottle of wine. "I sure wish she hadn't poisoned that," she said to no one in particular. "Because I sure could use a good shot of liquid courage right now."

"Just try," Cedric said as she turned to him. "'Tis true what Marc said. The princess is mine. And she just risked her life tae save us. The least we can do is the same for her."

Marc went to stand behind his mate, laying his hands upon her shoulders, giving her support. Cedric could see the bond between them, even if he couldn't feel it, and he longed for the same with his whole soul.

He could have that kind of a bond. He just had to go get her. "I'm ready."

With an anxious glance over her shoulder at Marc, Bronaugh took a deep breath, closed her eyes and lifted her hands.

Cedric watched as her image began to sparkle, then fade, and then grow stronger and stronger still.

Marc whispered something in her ear and colors shot out from all around her. But when she opened her eyes, they had gone completely black.

Cedric stuck in a breath, scared now that he had asked too much of her. That he had gone too far and she was gone to the dark side and would never get back. He opened his mouth to tell her to stop, but before he could utter a word, he was suddenly tumbling heels over arse, ice-cold wind whipping around him as he tumbled through a black abyss, unseen forces pulling him one way and then another. Unable to control the change, it burst through, his bones broke, his muscles tore, and his canines tore through his gums, shifting into his wolf as he tumbled through the air.

He landed hard, his large body punching a hole through grass and dirt. Panicked, he got his paws beneath him and leaped out of the hole.

Where the fook am I?

At first, he thought he was still in the abyss. But then his eyes adjusted to the darkness.

All around him was what appeared to be green grass and towering evergreens. A low growl rumbled in his throat. At first, he thought Bronaugh had just sent him somewhere into the forest.

But then he began to notice subtle differences.

A thick fog rolled over the ground, obscuring the world around him. Sniffing the air, he smelled pine and dirt, insects and some kind of animal.

But he heard no birds. No wind. Nothing.

His nerves on edge, Cedric threw back his head and howled into the silence. Wanting to fight someone. Something. Fucking anything.

As the echoes of his cry faded back into silence, he stood listening. Getting his bearings.

The human part of him wanted to panic, but his wolf knew that wouldn't get them anywhere. So, he tuned into his instincts.

Duana.

He had to find her.

Lifting his snout, he sniffed, searching for the faintest whiff of Snowdrops. He caught nothing in the still air, but he knew she was here. He could feel it in his bones.

Closing his eyes, he released the last of his human vestiges and gave everything up to his wolf. Listening to his instincts. Trying to get a lead on which direction to go.

Finally, his head whipped to the right. He didn't know what it was that had alerted him, but something was telling him to go that way. Without hesitation, he began to run. There was no sense in shifting back to his human form. He could cover more miles with less effort this way. And he had a better chance of taking on whatever this world threw at him.

Plus, he would blend into the inky darkness better in this form.

Cedric ran silently through the trees for what felt like days, but may have been seconds or hours in this strange world, when he saw a light flickering in the distance and smelled the smoke of a fire.

Quickly, he moved in that direction. When he got a little bit closer, he heard voices. Slowing down to a walk, he crept through the underbrush, damp from the heavy fog. As he got closer, the hackles rose on the back of his neck. He smelled something that reminded him of rotting meat.

Cedric knew where he was. He was in the world of the Dark Fae. A dimension that paralleled his own, but one that was full of magics he could never have imagined before he'd met their kind.

Lowering his belly to the ground, he crept closer to the fire, placing each large paw purposefully and silently, so as not to alert anyone of his presence. When he got close enough to see clearly through the trees, he stopped. A soft whine escaped before he could stop it.

A group of about seven male faeries and three females surrounded a small fire. They all wore human clothes, and they all had shaved heads and orange eyes, although some of them looked healthier than others.

Six of them had a dark "V" tattooed on their foreheads.

But that wasn't what had caused his emotions to escape him.

Duana hung above the fire, suspended in a bubble of magic very much like the sorcery he'd seen come out of Bronaugh. His princess was beaten and bloody, arms and legs spread wide, suspended by invisible ropes. But by the yellowish spots on her skin, he could tell she was already beginning to heal.

Reassured she was safe, for now, he cocked his ears and listened to the quiet argument going on around the fire.

"She is the princess," one of them said. Cedric couldn't

pinpoint exactly who, as his back was to him. "She's our leader. We should not be holding her like this."

The largest one didn't so much as turn his head to respond. "She is not my princess," he said. "She abandoned us. Went to the other world and stayed there after the war, instead of coming back here with us."

"Like her brother?" One of the females asked. "He was killed trying to get through before the portal locked."

"The crazy prince was the only one who could get us the hell out of here," a shorter male said.

"Yes, and now he's dead. And she killed him." The leader kicked at something on the ground—Cedric saw a head of long, white hair—then pointed up at Duana. "By that one action alone, it proves she has abandoned us. There's no way we'll get out of here now."

"Maybe she didn't have a choice," another one said. "The prince was dead when they got here."

"Poisoned," the leader said. "I can smell it on him, and she was the only one with him."

"She did not deny doing it." This came from the male at the end who'd been quiet until now.

"And how are we to kill her?" A female spoke up from the opposite side of the fire. "Between all of us we can barely contain her." She pointed up to the princess floating above them in the bubble. "She is weak right now because we managed to sneak up on her. But mark my words when I say, we will not be able to do it again. And when she gets out of there—which she will eventually—we are all dead."

"That's why we have to kill her first," the leader said.

"But we can get out now," the older female said. "The portal is opening."

He gave her a look of such disgust, Cedric could feel a wave of protectiveness for the strange female. "If you think the wolves will let that happen, the wolves that put us here to begin with, you're out of your fucking mind."

"They can't close the portal," she argued. "We have a chance to escape."

"No," the older female said. "They can't. But The Key can, and she is in that world."

"I heard rumors she had died," the short male said.

Aye, Cedric thought to himself. She did. But her daughter is verra much alive and is closing the portal as we speak.

"What are we going to do with the princess?"

As they continued to argue amongst themselves, Cedric began to creep around the outskirts of the small clearing, searching for a way to get to Duana. His entire body ached, muscles tensed and ready to charge in there at the first opportunity to save his mate.

On silent paws he crept closer. He knew he was taking a chance. They could detect him at any moment, and there was no way he could fight off all ten Dark Fae.

He needed a distraction. Something to get their attention so he could get to Duana and release her. There was no time to wait for them to wander off to bed. The clock was ticking.

He crept as close as he dared, thanking the gods for his black fur. He was close enough now she would see him there if she bothered to look, and Cedric willed her to do so with everything inside of him.

A few seconds later her head rolled on her neck and her eyes fluttered open. His heart squeezed painfully in his chest when he saw the inner proof of what they had done. Her beautiful, warm brandy eyes, full of pain, were now the color of mud.

Cedric waited, praying she would see him there. He knew the exact moment she did when he finally saw a flash of pink, then green, purple and blue. The colors sputtered and died, and then flickered back to life. And this time, they held steady as she stared right at him.

He nearly howled with joy.

She looked down at the faeries around the fire, and then back at him. Her eyes widened in fear and she shook her head, just enough for him to see.

"And who will lead us?" Someone called out.

"I will," the leader told them. "I've been doing it all this time while she's been playing in the human world."

"But what about—?"

He held up his hand, halting her before she could finish. "This conversation is over," he said. "Bring her down."

Seven members of the group stepped forward raised their hands toward the princess. Orange light that matched their eyes extended from their fingertips, like bolts of lightning. They each took a part of the bubble, lowering it down to the ground and holding it there.

Cedric watched and waited. She needed to be free of the magic before he could do anything to save her. If not, she could be stuck in the bubble until her powers came back while he got himself killed, which was the most likely outcome. But at least he would die trying to save the female he loved.

And even if by some miracle he didn't get himself killed, he didn't understand enough about their magic to know if she would be able to get out if the ones who put her in the bubble were dead.

So, he waited and he watched. He knew he wouldn't have much time. Once they released her, they would be on her fast. He would have a split second. Maybe less.

They argued amongst themselves for another minute until the leader finally screamed at them to be quiet. Lifting his arm he directed his magic toward the bubble, ripping a hole right through the center of it. Cedric felt his heart leap within his chest for a moment, afraid the magic had sliced right through the princess. But it didn't. The bubble broke apart, sparkling brighter than the stars for a few seconds before dissipating and rising up to join their brothers and sisters in the sky.

Time stopped as the magic around her floated away. Yet, for a moment she hung suspended before falling hard to the ground.

Lying on the cold, wet ground, Cedric stayed perfectly still. But his mind was racing, thinking up different scenarios and tossing them aside just as quickly as they appeared. Over and over he kept coming to the same conclusion...

There was no way they were going to make it out of there alive.

His eyes traveled over his princess, a bright light in the dark sky. A female full of fire and passion who fought him at every turn, who cared for her people, and who had killed her own father. To save him.

So be it.

He dug his claws into the dirt, leaning his weight back on his hind legs, preparing to pounce...

Duana's colorful eyes flashed in warning as he rose up off the ground.

Teeth bared, he growled loud and deep. His plan to distract them just long enough for the princess to get away.

All eyes turned toward him in surprise…

A glowing blue fire roared across the clearing. Cedric jumped back just in time as it singed his fur. In horror, he watched as Duana was consumed by the flames with the others.

Throwing his head back, he howled in anguish as his heart burst inside his chest. Over and over until his voice was raw in his throat.

And then one of the faeries raced from the flames, unhurt.

As soon as the flames receded, he raced back into the fray where he had last seen the princess. He found her lying on the ground, her body unscathed but the wind was knocked out of her. Her eyes shifted to him. "Get me out of here, wolf," she whispered.

Careful not to cut her skin and cause her more injury, he took her arm in his mouth and dragged her away from the chaos.

Once they were out of the way, he lowered himself to the ground beside her. She didn't complain. Didn't say she couldn't do it. But he heard her hiss of pain as he felt one arm and one leg get thrown over his back. She gripped his fur with one hand and pulled herself slowly and painfully over his back.

As soon as her weight was distributed evenly across his body, he disappeared into the underbrush, trying to jiggle her as little as possible. He felt her moan and tuck her face into the side of his neck to protect it from the thorns and branches, but there was nothing he could about the rest of her.

His mind focused on getting them the hell away from the war that was breaking out, he had no idea how to get them back home. But for right now, just getting them somewhere

where they could stop and think and heal would be a good start.

"Hurry! This way!"

The voice came from his left, and Cedric's head whipped around, his muzzle lifted, baring his teeth in a fierce snarl.

"Stop growling at me or I'm going to leave your ass here," Bronaugh told him.

Cedric searched the trees around her.

"Marc's not here. He's waiting. We have to go." She ran off a little ways and hurled an electric ball into the trees on the other side of the fire. Those left standing quickly focused on that spot. "Let's go!"

He swung his head to the side, trying to see Duana.

"Run, wolf," she whispered.

And he did.

CHAPTER 20

Cedric awoke us up drifting up from a dream. The back of his skull pounded and his body was wrapped around the princess. Unclenching his jaw, he wasn't surprised to see he had even held onto her with his teeth, biting down on the muscle between her neck and shoulder until he tasted blood.

From the dim light filtering into the cave through a small hole in the ceiling, he would guess the sun was setting in the sky. He didn't know how long they'd been there, but as he relaxed his jaw and loosened his arms and legs from around her, she stirred above him and lifted her weight from his chest.

"What the hell were you doing there? You could have been trapped in there with me."

"I'd rather be trapped in your world with ye than live in my own without ye." Cedric now understood why Brock was the way he was with Heather. So possessive and protective, not wanting her to leave his side, even for a second.

Colors flashed in her eyes. "I've been so horrible to you."

"Aye, ye have."

"And yet, you came after me anyway."

"I will always come after ye, kitten."

"I don't know that I deserve such loyalty. But I hope what you just said is true, because..." She paused, the hues of her eyes dimming with uncertainty.

"Because wha'?" Cedric brushed her long locks back from her face. "Please tell me, Duana. I need tae hear it."

Slowly, her eyes returned to his. "Because I think I love you, wolf. I think I am falling in love with you. And it terrifies the hell out of me, even as I long for you with every beat of my heart."

Her face blurred before him. Cedric blinked rapidly, desperately trying to hold on to this moment. Declarations such as this did not come easy to his mate, this he knew, so when they came, he wanted to treasure each one. "Thank ye, lass." His voice was rough with emotion.

Her eyes traveled over his face, like she was memorizing his features, and then Duana started to get up.

"Where are ye going, lass? he asked her, sitting up. Chills chased each other across his bare skin as he brushed his hair from his eyes, now that the heat of her was gone.

She didn't answer.

"Dinna think yer going tae run away, princess," he teased her. "I traveled all the way tae yer world tae find ye. Ye are mine now."

"The portal is closing."

For the first time, Cedric turned to give their surroundings a good look. They were deep in a rock cave, somewhere behind a waterfall by the sound of it. He followed her stare.

Blue light crackled in the air, like a spider's web. As he watched, it folded in on itself, condensing until he could hardly see the separate strands. It grew smaller and smaller, until it was the size of a basketball.

"Where is Bronaugh?" He looked around. Searching for her blonde hair. "Bronaugh!"

"She's here." Duana pointed to the left. Bronaugh lay by a large boulder, curled around it like a lover.

"Is she...?" He couldn't say it.

"She's fine."

His eyes were drawn back to Duana, her sorrow a more powerful draw than his worry. "Och, lass."

As they watched, the lightening tightened into a ball the size of a quarter, dimmed, then went black.

Duana's chin fell to her chest and a sob escaped her.

Cedric was on his feet and pulling her into his arms before it had fully disappeared. "I'm so verra sorry, kitten."

"It's not your fault," she told him. Lifting her head from his chest, she gave him a watery smile. "Thank you for coming to save me."

"Och, aye." He hugged her close.

They stood like that for a long time, taking comfort from one another. When Cedric felt her heartbeat calm and her breathing even out, he brushed her hair back from her eyes and lifted her face to his.

She closed her eyes. Whether it was because she didn't want him to see her tears or because she knew he was about to kiss her, he didn't know. But he was quickly growing attached to her Fae ways. "Do no' close yer bonnie eyes," he whispered. "For I've never seen such a beautiful sight."

Slowly, they fluttered open. "Truly?" she asked.

"Aye," he confirmed.

A tear slipped down her cheek and he wiped it away with

his thumb. "Dinna be so sad, kitten. There are still many o' yer people already here who need tae be saved with yer herbs."

"And you'll let me do it?"

"Aye," he told her. "If it will keep ye busy and out o' my hair."

She narrowed her eyes, and he grinned in the face of her annoyance.

"But I'll only give ye six months tae come up with a cure, or we wolves will do what we need tae do."

"You're giving me a time limit?"

"Aye. I feel I need tae. For the safety o' all."

"But by that time, you'll have them all rounded up and they won't be able to hurt anyone, anyway."

"And what if one escapes?"

"They won't escape."

"How do ye ken? It might."

"My people are not an 'it'," she stated in a firm voice.

"They are no' yer people when the addiction takes them," he insisted.

"Yes, they are."

"No, they are no'."

She opened her mouth, and Cedric took that as the perfect invitation to end the argument.

Lowering his head, he took her mouth with his, wrapping her luscious body in his arms and pulling her tight against him. His cock swelled, hurting to be inside of her, and he found he was just as anxious to feel their souls join. If he was going to die, he wanted it to be the deathless death he felt in her arms.

When his kisses forced the anger from her body and she was clinging to him in desperation instead, he asked, "Are ye ever going tae stop fighting with me?"

"I would think not."

"Aye," he said with a happy grin. "Good."

Lifting her in his arms, he carried her deeper into the cave, away from Bronaugh and any rescue party who may happen to find them.

* * *

THANK YOU FOR READING! I hope you loved reading Cedric and Duana's story. If you need more shifters, read Fire of the Dreki now.

Kohl Sergones knows there's no place for a woman around a creature like him—half vampire, half dragon, and the only one of his kind. The dragon senses Devon before Kohl does, and it awakens with a burning hunger he can't ignore…

Click here to read Fire of the Dreki now!

"Oh Kohl, Kohl, Kohl... Seriously guys Kohl. He is one of my all time favorite alpha males." - Megan M.-Amazon reviewer.

"What do you get when you cross a dragon shifter with a vampire? Kohl, you get Kohl! I loved loved this book - in fact once I started reading it, I didn't stop until I had finished. Who needs sleep right?" Chrissi-Amazon reviewer.

ABOUT THE AUTHOR

L.E. Wilson writes romance starring intense alpha males and the women who are fearless enough to tame them — for the most part anyway. ;) In her novels you'll find smoking hot scenes, a touch of suspense, some humor, a bit of gore, and multifaceted characters, all working together to combine her lifelong obsession with the paranormal and her love of romance.

Her writing career came about the usual way: on a dare from her loving husband. Little did she know just one casual suggestion would open a box of worms (or words as the case may be) that would forever change her life.

Lattes and music are a necessary part of her writing

process, though sometimes you'll find her typing away at her favorite Starbucks. She walks two miles to get there, to make up for all of those coffees.

On a Personal Note:

"I love to hear from my readers! Contact me anytime at le@lewilsonauthor.com."

Keep In Touch With L.E.
lewilsonauthor.com
le@lewilsonauthor.com